Avalonia

First Edition

Published by Faith by Grace Publishing

First Faith by Grace Publishing Printing 2014.

ISBN-13: 978-0692560136

ISBN-10: 0692560130

A record of the Library of Congress serial number can be acquired from the publisher.

Manufactured in the United States of America

Cover Photo by Amber Kincaid

I would like to dedicate this book
to my wonderful Husband.

Table of Contents

Part I

Part II

Part III

PART I

Chapter 1

My parents once told me the story of how they met. It was in a truly unusual way.

One day, while my father was out with his werewolf pack, checking the borders of their vast Packlands, they came across a coven of vampires, who, they later learned, had been chased from their home by another coven. These vampires were walking in daylight. The wolves had heard of such a coven, but had never actually met them. It was believed that they were blessed by a witch, over a hundred years ago, when they saved her life. Of course, the two groups were wary of each other, at first, being natural born enemies, but then my father, the Alpha, saw her. My mother. His mate.

My father had waited almost sixty years to meet her, and here she was. A glorious creature. Who, in all aspects, was the complete opposite of him. She had raven black hair, in contrast to his silver-white locks. Her eyes were dark brown, his were bright green. Her short, at only 5' 5", and him standing at an impressive 6' 10". Which, even for werewolves, is quite tall.

"What, may I ask, are you doing on my lands?" He asked, trying to contain the excitement that he felt.

My mother who was the oldest, most respected vampire of the coven, and thus their Súmaire, or leader, answered, "We have been run from our lands by another coven. They say our land is larger and better than theirs. They have killed a lot of my coven. We are just looking for a new place to call home. We have not travelled outside of our lands in a long time. We were looking for Astoria, the capital city. All we want is safe passage through your land."

My father started shaking. How dare someone harm his mate. His... He did not know her name.

"What is your name?" He inquired, trying to calm himself down.

"Melovanin." She replied, sweetly. "And yours?"

"Donovan." He replied. He looked around at his pack before saying. "I will allow you to stay on my land for the night. We shall discuss future arrangements for your coven after dinner."

He turned and headed back toward his house. Both pack and coven followed.

As they arrived, the coven looked around in amazement. The place was huge. It was a lot bigger than where the coven used to live, in a mansion, a few miles outside the pack borders, in the Vampire Lands. The main pack house stood in the center of the grounds. On one side stood the pack hospital. On the other, smaller houses branched out and formed a circle. Connecting back to the hospital. My father smiled as he saw their looks of appreciation. He gave them a moment, then told his men to show the coven where they could stay. Melovanin started to follow, he grabbed her arm.

"Melo...." He started.

She interjected. "Mel. I prefer to be called Mel."

He smiled slightly. "Mel it is, then." He said. "I would like to speak with you, before dinner, if that would be alright."

She smiled. She had a hunch about what he was going to say. My father did not know that vampires, like werewolves, could sense their soul mates. She knew it was him, from the moment she saw him. She just needed to be sure he wouldn't reject her. Which, from what she had been told, was the most painful thing anyone could ever experience.

"Okay. Lead on." She said.

He led her to his office. It was attached to the master bedroom and was one of the larger rooms in the house. The pack house was a grand, three story mansion that had fifty bedrooms, three living rooms, two kitchens, and thirty bathrooms. Not counting the ballroom, numerous closets, and offices.

As soon as they entered, my father closed the door.

"I know this may be hard for you to understand," He began, " but us werewolves have what we call soul mates. It is someone who is made just for us. We know who they are, as soon as we see them. That is, after our nineteenth birthday. From that moment on, no one else matters." He paused, getting somewhat puzzled by the half smile that was playing at her lips. "You are mine." He finished. He stared at her. Waiting for her to freak out.

Instead, she began to laugh. Not a little chuckle, but a full on laugh. This puzzled him even more.

"What is so funny?" He asked, slightly taken aback.

"You think...vampires...don't have...soul mates!?!" She tried to say, through the laughter and tears.

"You do? But we were always told we were the only ones who could recognize our soul mates." He said. The look on his face was one of pure confusion.

She began to calm down, not because she didn't find it funny anymore, but because she knew she needed to answer him. To tell him why no one knew vampires could sense their mates, as well.

"Vampires, like werewolves, can sense their mates. We just do not act upon it until we have a chance to see how they react to us. Not everyone is so accepting of vampires." She paused and looked at him. She hoped the next words that she said would not offend him. "Especially werewolves." My father grimaced when she said it, but he knew it was true. They had been enemies for too long for there not to be any tension.

"Many of our race end up rejected. That is why we do not like for others to know." She continued, "If they are unaware that we know who they are to us, then the decision is truly theirs. It's not a choice made from a feeling of guilt, because they do not want to face the pain we would be in. It is better for all if they go on believing we can not sense our soul mates."

My father just stared at her. Then nodded his head slightly. It made sense to him. They, in a way, we're trying to protect their soul mates. They were leaving the decision truly up to them. No guilt involved. He had known quite a few wolves who had been guilted into mating before they were ready and it never ended well.

He smiled at her. "I completely understand, but why did you laugh at me when I was telling you all that. I mean if I am not supposed to know, then how is it funny that I didn't?"

"Back in the old days, all alpha werewolves were told. It allowed them to handle situations where one of their pack was mated to a vampire better. They could help the wolf get to the point of accepting his mate fully, so that it would never be a true rejection. I just assumed they still did that. I am sorry I laughed at you, Donovan." She stated softly, her eyes beginning to tear up. She did not want to make her mate upset.

He saw the tears right away and ran to her. He did not want her to cry and couldn't figure out why she was. Then it dawned on him, she thought he was mad because she had laughed.

He held her until she eventually calmed down. He grabbed her face gently and stared into her eyes.

"There is no need to cry, my dear. I am not angered with you." He said lovingly. "I accept you as my mate. And, I hope that you accept me, as well."

"I do. I, so, do." She said.

"Great! Then, it is settled! Do you mind if I inform my pack over dinner?" He asked, hoping she said yes. He was so excited that he didn't think he could wait one more minute to tell his pack.

"Yes, you may. But I need to speak to my coven about this. I know you want to talk to them, after dinner, about arrangements for the future, but I am their leader, and I need to find a land for them, so that they can move on and carve out a new home for themselves." She answered. She knew it would be hard for the coven to stay with the pack. There would be conflict since the two were, historically, enemies.

"I would like for them to stay here, if they wish. I know our kinds don't normally mix, but they are your family, and I want you to be happy. If they are far away, you would not be." He said. "So, will you ask them that, before you decide to elect a new leader?" He asked.

She beamed up at him. His heart skipped a beat.

"Yes," She replied, "I would be happy to. Thank you."

"You're welcome." He stated.

They spent the next hour talking about anything and everything. Just getting to know each other. Then my mother had to leave, to speak with the coven. While she was away, my father paced across his office. He was losing it. He had only known her for a few hours and he already could not stand to be away from her.

My mother had been the Súmaire of the coven for a very long time, almost one hundred years. The coven went into an uproar when my mother first told them of her mate. They didn't want to lose her. But, when she told them the offer her mate had laid on the table, they all drew silent. Neither option seemed pleasant to them. They had to decide. Life with werewolves, who most of them despised, or life without their beloved Súmaire. In the end, the choice was simple.

That night, at dinner, as the pack and coven dined, my father was restless. He was trying to wait until the end of dinner to tell the pack, but, with his beautiful mate so close, and considering the stares she was getting, it was hard. In the end, he could wait no longer. He banged on his glass to get their attention.

"My pack, and our guests, I have a very important announcement." He beamed at everyone there. Most of the pack had never seen him smile like that. "I have found my mate. Your Luna."

The entire room burst into applause and cheers. Finally, it calmed enough for him to speak.

"I would like to introduce, my beautiful mate, Melovanin." He said, while holding out his hand to her.

The room went silent. Nothing could be heard. No one expected a vampire. It was very rare for mates to be interspecies and most, that were, did not end up together. It took a few moments for it to sink in. Their Alpha had found his mate, and he had accepted her, even if she was a vampire, so they would too. At that moment, their species did not matter. The room, once more, filled with cheers.

Chapter 2

It took my parents almost ten years to have me. During that time they lived peacefully. Both coven and pack had learned to coincide with each other.

I was born on a stormy winter's night. Pack and coven were rushing around together, trying to gather all the things they needed for my birth. I was coming three weeks early. Nothing was ready, but, through it all, my mother stayed calm. She knew everything was going to be alright.

My father, on the other hand, was a mess. He had just gotten back from the borders, where a group of humans were trying to cross. Humans were not allowed on our lands, nor we on theirs. It was a law that had just been passed the previous year, along with separate school systems, everyone now had their own. The law was passed in the name of safety. It seemed humans had been getting hurt and killed way too often back then.

By the time I made my appearance, everything had calmed down. I was an exact mix of my parents, with bright green eyes and raven black hair. The doctor, a witch, made it just in time. Witch doctors were common in mixed births because they are able to tell what species a baby is, as soon as it is born, saving the interspecies families a lot of waiting around and worry.

As I arrived, everyone was waiting patiently for the doctor to tell them whether I was a wolf or a vampire. But all the doctor did was stare and mumble, "No, this can't be." Over and over again. My father grew worried.

"What is wrong with my daughter, Doctor?" He practically growled.

"Oh, what?" He mumbled. When finally he caught on to what was asked, he looked up. "There is nothing really...wrong with your daughter, sir. It's just.." He ran a hand down over his face while trying to think of the right words to describe something he had never seen, or even heard about, before.

"WHAT IS IT?!" My father shouted, loud enough for the entire pack and coven to hear.

"She is both." He simply stated.

My mother gasped, then asked, "What do you mean both?!"

The doctor took another look at me, while saying, "I have never seen it before, but somehow your daughter is both werewolf and vampire. She is some sort of hybrid."

"You must have done the spell wrong! That isn't possible!" My mother said, as she started to cry.

"But she is healthy, right? There is nothing physically wrong with her?" My father asked.

"Not at all," the doctor stated, "She is healthy, and really quite remarkable. The first of a new species!"

My father came and picked me up, taking me to my mother.

"I do not care that she is 'both'. She is ours and I will love her the same!" He said.

My mother looked at him gratefully. "Me, too." She stated softly, but firmly.

"We will have to inform the Council about her." The doctor said.

My father flinched. Even though he was the Alpha of his pack, the Council ruled over all. They are the ones who decided the fate of every living creature. The most powerful elders of each species held a seat at the Council. No one could go against them.

"I know." My father said. "I know."

It was a week later that they finally went to see the Council. At first, they marveled on how such a creature as me could exist, but after a while they got down to business. Word had spread throughout all the packs and covens, and even into the Human Lands, of the hybrid baby. Some were joyous, but most were terrified. They couldn't wrap their minds around a new species.

Chapter 3

My early childhood was great. I grew up with parents, a pack, and coven, who taught me that I could be anything that I wanted to be and do anything I wanted to do. I had everything I could ever want or wish for.

That all changed the year I turned five. I was to start school the August before my fifth birthday, but, since all werewolves change on their fifth birthday, it was decided that I would start in January.

My birthday party was amazing. My parents went all-out. I received extravagant gifts, and everyone that I loved was in attendance.

That was the night of my *change*. Since I was a hybrid, no one knew how it would affect me. I will say, now, looking back, that it was the worst pain that I have ever felt.

The *change* itself was not bad, it was what came after. My vampire emerged too, earlier than expected. Since both parts were so new to me, I could not control either one. It was like a raging battle was going on inside me. **They** both wanted to be dominate. **They** both wanted control. If my vampire would not have came forward so early, it could have been different. My wolf would have had her day of freedom and in turn may have allowed my vampire hers.

The pain from this brutal internal assault lasted days. In the end, neither side won. **They** both tired and called a truce.

Another thing no one expected was my powerful violent streak. After the *change*, anytime I pulled my vampire, or werewolf, or both, forward I became deadly. Both sides relished in the fear **they** could cause. **They** loved the screams. My human side, though, could not stand it. I was lucky all werewolves were born with a human side, as well as a wolf. If not, I would have been even deadlier. I never understood how **they** could be so violent. I had no control. I was too young to rein in a force that powerful.

A week after my *change,* I was playing with a few of the children from my pack. The pack still trusted and loved me, even though I had became a monster. We had been playing hide and seek. It was a way for all of us to strengthen our Werewolf abilities and, for me, my Vampire abilities. Everything was going well, my hybrid seemed happy for the first time, until **we** were found. The child who found **us** seemed to forget about my *change*. He started taunting. He laughed at **us**. He was so happy that he had found **us**. My hybrid would not stand for this. I *changed* and attacked. The other kids screamed. The kid was lucky that there was an adult nearby. I was pulled off of him. There was blood everywhere. My hybrid was laughing. By this time, the rest of the pack and coven had arrived, as well as my parents. They took one look at the child, then to me. My mother and father carefully took me into their arms and pulled me away from the pack and coven. That night I was taken to the Council. There was no way for my parents to get out of taking me. The pack and coven would not stand for my lack of control. Next time, I could kill one of them.

For most of the next two years, the Council locked me up in a prison cell in the capital city of Astoria. It was the center of all the lands. Every species was able to travel into Astoria, but not into the other lands.

It had taken a lot of persuasion from my parents for me to just be detained. I had been losing control more and more. I began attacking any animal I came across. The Council believed it was only a matter of time before I would attack another child. The Council wanted me dead.

The werewolf Council member, Carter, convinced them to lock me up and study me, instead. He did not want to waste an opportunity. Another hybrid may never be born. During my captivity they ran many tests. They were trying to figure out how I was what I was and, also, if I could be of any use to them. They wanted to know if they could create more like me. The tests they ran were extensive. Ranging from simple blood work to having me *change*. Sometimes just into my wolf, other times my vampire, but mainly pulling both forth at the same time. The Council was fascinated by the fact that I had two dominating forces inside of me. They wanted to harness it. They wanted to replicate it.

I had always, before this, pulled **them** forward together. Since **they** had emerged together, I did not think it was possible to pull **them** forward separately. I had only been locked up a week when the Council made me try. I was in a cell that was encased, on all sides but one, with mirrors. The fourth side was for the Council to watch me and was made of glass. It took me days to learn how to control *it*. Finally, I *changed* only into my wolf. I became fully a wolf. My face elongated. My hands changed into paws. I landed, not so gracefully, on all fours. I looked like every other werewolf child. My vampire was easier. When

I tried to pull her forward, by herself, she came easily. My fangs grew. My eyes turned black. These were the only indications that I had changed. Changing into my hybrid was the easiest of all. I had been doing that since my birthday. When I pulled **them** both forward, my ears elongated. My fangs grew. My nails changed into claws. My eyes blackened. My facial features changed slightly. Hair sprouted out on the sides of my face. My nose grew slightly. The Council was amazed at all of this. They did not understand how one child could do all of this.

My parents spent every day training me while I was locked up in Astoria. They worked hours on end, so that I could finally control the monsters within me. I had a handle on **them,** but **they** still loved the screams and fear. I had to learn to live with **them**. I hated what I was, even at seven years old, but there was nothing I could do to change it. Finally, one month after my seventh birthday, I was released.

The parents of the other children were afraid to have me in the same school as their children. Homeschooling was out of the question. My parents had way too many responsibilities as Alpha and Luna. They had relied too heavily on the pack and coven the past two years, as they were taking care of me, they could no longer do that and keep their positions. It was decided, by the Council, to appease all the Vampire and Werewolf parents, and so that they, the Council, could keep an eye on me, that I would go to the Human Lands and blend in there. No one there would know who I was. What I was. The only way for that to work, though, was if they never found out. If they did, either they, or I, would be killed. More than likely they would. The Council still hadn't studied me enough.

Finally, after all my years in captivity, I was ready to begin my journey in the Human Lands.

Chapter 4

My parents escorted me to the border of the Human Lands. Even though the Council was forcing me to attend the human schools, my parents were still not allowed into their lands. Michael, the human Council member, met us there. He was a short, chubby man with mousy brown hair and glasses, that he was constantly adjusting on his face. He wore a brown suit, that closely matched his hair. From the first moment that I met him, **they** wanted to tear him apart. He was the first human that I had contact with. All **they** could think about was how he would taste. **They** wanted to taste his blood. His flesh. It took all my strength not to do just that.

"I will be watching over Avalonia until she is old enough to do it herself. I understand that you will be arranging places for her to live, after that point?" He inquired.

My father answered, while holding my crying mother, "Yes, we will. Carter gave us the names of all the realtors in your lands. Just tell us where she will be going and we will find a safe place for her to stay." As Carter's name was mentioned, I couldn't help but let out a small growl. I hated him. He had been the one who had made me do the tests. He is the one who had me tortured by making me change my forms everyday. Some of the things he made me go through, I still refuse to speak of, to this day. My parents sent me a look, but were too worried about me leaving to really reprimand me.

"Please, take care of her. She is all we have!" My mother cried out, then buried her head in my father's shirt once more.

"I will do my best to ensure that she stays safe and out of trouble." He said, while turning toward me. "Come along, Avalonia. We have a long way to travel, today."

I hugged my parents one last time, not knowing when I would see them again, and followed Michael to his car. I was scared. How would I handle the urges without their guidance? They had been there constantly to help me. Now, I would have to try and handle it on my own.

Once we arrived at the house we would be staying in, Michael showed me to my room. It was huge compared to the cell I had been in the past few years. I loved it. I loved the entire house. He informed me that we would be having dinner in an hour. Then it would be time for bed, since I was to start school the following day.

After dinner, as I was getting ready for bed, I could not help but to think of what these humans would be like. How would they react to a new student and how would I react to them? Besides Michael, I had never been around a human and, since I had wanted to tear him apart, it didn't bode well for the others. I feared how my wolf and my vampire would react. It took me hours to fall asleep that night and, once I did, it was not restful. I dreamed of ripping humans limb from limb and gorging on meat and blood. I awoke in a cold sweat. I didn't even try to go back to sleep. I knew it would be pointless.

The next morning, as Michael was driving me to school, he started to explain the rules of the human school to me. As if I had not heard them enough over the two years I had been locked up.

"Avalonia, in this school you will not be able to shift, or show any type of supernatural abilities. They do not know about you and they can not know. You may make friends. But, be warned, if they get suspicious, we will either have to move you or have them killed. Maybe even both, if they try to tell anyone. Do you understand?" He asked.

"Yes," I replied, still thinking of my dream from the previous night. Would I even dare make friends?

Once we arrived, he walked me in and introduced me as his 'niece, from a few towns over' to the principal. The principal was a middle aged man with a fading hair line and a huge round belly. He seemed nice enough. I didn't want to rip him apart, at least. Michael left as the principal guided me to what would be my classroom. He knocked on the door and a woman, whom I presumed was my new teacher, came out. She was lovely. Light golden hair and beautiful blue eyes. As with the principal, I didn't have the urge to rip her apart. I still wanted to scare them, make them fear me, but, for the moment, not to kill.

"Hello, Mr. Walters. What can I do for you?" She asked the principal, while glancing at me.

"I have a new student that will be joining your class, Miss Toliver. This is Avalonia." He said, while slightly pushing me forward.

"It is a pleasure to meet you, Avalonia." She said, while extending her hand.

I took her hand like Michael showed me and tried to shake it as gently as possible. My wolf wanted to cause her pain. **She** wanted me to squeeze her hand hard. I had to push **her** down. It was by no means an easy task.

"It is nice to meet you, too." I said, as politely as possible, through gritted teeth. I was still straining to keep my wolf at bay.

She guided me into the classroom and stood me at the front. All of the children stopped talking and stared as we entered.

"Class this is our new student, Avalonia." She introduced. "Please, welcome her."

All of the kids began to wave and say 'hi'. My hybrid hated all the cheeriness. **They** wanted to cause fear. I had to force my nails into my hands to keep from changing into my hybrid and scaring them all. I took a moment to calm down and waved back at them, hoping my hands had healed before I did.

Vampires and Werewolves healed faster than humans. If a werewolf and human both cut their hand, the Werewolves would heal within a day, were the humans would take days. In comparison, Vampires heal almost instantaneously. Being half vampire, my hands healed completely within seconds.

"Avalonia, Please take a seat in front of Nancy." She instructed me, then turned to face the class. "Nancy, raise your hand please."

Once she did, I slowly walked to the seat in front of Nancy. She was a small girl with blonde hair and brown eyes.

"Hello, I'm Nancy." She said.

"Hi, I am Avalonia." I replied.

All throughout class Nancy chatted. She told me all about the school; where everything was, who was friends with whom, what classes we had, and so on. She also told me that she had no friends and would love it if I would be her friend. I was wary, of course, but I couldn't help but like her. So, I gave her a chance. My hybrid went along with it. **They** liked the idea of having someone to toy with.

Over the next three years, life for me pretty much stayed the same. The only exception was that, as time went on, I saw Michael less and less. He had Council business that kept him in Astoria. He started out skipping a dinner here and there, then he just stopped coming altogether. Now, at three years in, I only saw him on holidays and birthdays. He brought me presents from my parents. I was forced to grow up a lot during that time. I had not seen my parents since I had left them that day. The only contact I had with them was over the phone. Since Michael was away all the time, I had to take care of myself. There was no one else to rely on.

Though I had become very good friends with Nancy, she did not suspect my truth, at all. I loved having someone to call a friend, after my years in captivity. My hybrid had even gotten to the point that **they** stopped wanting just to toy with her and **they**, too, began to consider her a friend. Life was, finally, normal. That is, until Nancy stopped by unexpectedly.

I was home alone. I wasn't expecting anyone to stop by. I was using my vampire speed to do my chores, like always, when I saw something out of the corner of my eye. I went to the window and saw Nancy running away from the house, down the driveway. She had seen me! I was freaking out. I called the only people that I knew to call, my parents. They also freaked out. I did not think she would tell anyone, but we couldn't take the chance. My parents called Michael and the Council. The next day, I was moved. I have no clue what happened to Nancy, but I would never set foot in that town again.

Chapter 5

It took no time at all for me to get to a new town and settled into a new school. I decided this time that I would stay out of the way. I would make no friends. If I didn't have friends, there was less of a chance that anyone would find out.

The town that I moved to was surrounded by mountains. I had missed the mountains when I lived in the last town. Here I could go out and hike to remote locations, where others could not go. Instead of spending time with a friend, I was now spending everyday out in the wild. My wolf was ecstatic. She had not been out in a long time. Michael and the Council found a spot high up on the mountain for me. A private spot. So that I could *change* and not be found out, but, most importantly, so I would not be able to hurt anyone. I liked this town.

My wolf was wilder than ever. My vampire had, at least, gotten to come out weekly, when I did my chores. My wolf, never. **Her** instincts demanded that I spent every day up in the mountains. And, after a time, she finally grew happy, and somewhat content, in our new life.

The school here was a lot different than the last. The kids here were more violent. Everyday there was fighting. My two supernatural sides begged to be let out. **They** loved the screams. The pain. The fear. I hated it. I wanted to get away from that school.

I made it through the first year in that school with no problems. Not that it was easy. The beginning of the second year is when it went wrong. I was walking down the hall and not really paying attention, when I ran into one of the popular girls, Allison. She was your typical super preppy, blonde hair, bright blue eyed, cheerleader, and she hated anyone who wasn't popular.

"Watch where you are going!" She shouted, making sure everyone could hear.

"I am sorry." I mumbled. Trying not to let my wolf and vampire show. **They** were both enraged from being disrespected.

"You better be, you freak! I don't even know who you are, but I better never see you again or I will make you pay." She stated. While everyone else in the hall laughed. My eyes squinted. My nostrils flared. I was ready to tear her apart. I had to get away. Allison smirked wickedly. She loved the attention.

I ran straight home. It was such a close call. All I could think about, while she talked, was ripping her apart. I headed to the mountain. I needed to hunt. To feel flesh in my teeth. Blood in my throat. I needed to kill!

I returned to school a week later. Refreshed after taking the week off to hunt, both sides of me were satisfied. Happy even. But that feeling did not last long. As soon as I entered the school, I saw Allison and all the anger from the week before resurfaced. Luckily, after all the training that I had, I was able to push it down. Barely. I would just have to try to avoid her.

I managed to do that, for another two weeks. Then Allison, quite literally, ran into me as I was walking down the hallway at school. My wolf was on the verge of surfacing. **She** didn't like the intrusion. My vampire found my wolf funny. *She* was egging it on. *She* wanted to taste blood and knew if my wolf surfaced *she* would. I felt myself begin to *change*, It took all my strength to keep from doing so.

"I am... Oh, it's you again. I thought I told you to watch where you were going!" She stated loudly.

I was shaking from the strain of not *changing*. I was fighting a losing battle. I knew if I tried to talk it would come out as a growl. I just closed my eyes and started breathing deeply. Slowly calming myself down. That is when I felt it. She had hit me. This puny human dared to hit me! That was it. I was losing control and I couldn't stop it. She tried to hit me again, since she did not get the desired reaction the first time, I guess. I grabbed her arm forcefully. I could feel the bones creaking in my hand, they were on the verge of breaking. My wolf was elated.

She tried to pull her arm away. Her body squirming. I smiled as she fought. She was doing exactly what I wanted. Exactly what my hybrid needed. I tightened my grip even more. She grimaced. Her face contorted in pain. I could hear her faint whimpering. I was a moment away from ripping her arm off and finally getting what my hybrid so desperately wanted, when I heard...

"Avalonia! What do you think you are doing?!" It was Michael. He had come to the school to check in with me, since I had been absent from my classes, during the previous week. He arrived just in time. He saw my eyes. Saw what was happening. He had to act fast. He began reminding me of my training, coaxing me back into my own body. While, as gently and slowly as possible, so as not to startle my wolf, pulling her arm out of my grip. Once her arm was free, he had some students take her to the nurse. He knew he could not leave me alone. He knew I was on edge. A moment away from a complete transformation.

My hybrid fought every step of the way. **They** did not want to give up control. I lost track of what was going on around me. I focused solely on containing my monster. Somehow, I found myself outside. When I was finally in control and realized what I had done, I was a mess. How could I have let **them** take over. How could I have hurt someone.

Michael said that no one suspected anything. Why would they? At that school, fights were normal. They just thought I was another crazy girl. Someone who needed to be avoided. Allison's arm had, thankfully, just been severely sprained at the wrist. Any human could have done that to her. I didn't need to leave, but how could I stay? I couldn't see her all the time. I would never forgive myself. Also, my hybrid would try to take over, try to finish what **they** started. The risk was too large.

That is how I found myself packing my bags and moving again.

Over the next six years, I moved around a lot. I switched schools at least once a year. Sometimes twice. I made sure to stay out of everyone's way. I had Michael set up my classes so that there would be as few kids as possible in each one. I waited until the hallways cleared before going to each class. That way I wouldn't run into anyone.

During that time, I had grown up a lot. I had managed to gain better control of my wolf and vampire. Not fully, but pretty close. At least, I no longer felt the instinct to kill someone for running into me. I would still feel like dismembering a disrespectful peer, on occasion, but that was just the way I was designed. Cursed to a life where parts of me longed, and thrived, for pain and fear.

My human side would never be happy, but, from what I have seen, not many humans are.

Eventually, I left for what I hoped would be my last human school.

PART II

Chapter 6

It was a stormy night. All that could be heard was the rain softly hitting the tin roof. It was set up to be one of the most relaxing nights that I would have had in awhile, but I still could not relax.

My mind was racing. My heart pounding. I was afraid. Afraid that they would find out.

They were already growing suspicious. I mean who wouldn't be. This strange, new girl who disappears randomly and appears just the same. They would never understand why I have to do what I do. No one could.

I had just moved to this town the month before. I tried to lay low, like always. Stay out of the way, be a fly on the wall. It's not that I didn't want to make friends here. I just didn't have the option.

I began to notice something odd, about a week after I got to this new school. A few of the students seemed to be around me all the time. I tried to ignore it, at first, but they were persistent. One day they approached.

"Hello, my name is Samantha." The girl in the red shirt, who seemed to be the leader of the group, said. "This is Carly and Tammy," She introduced the other two. Who seemed to be wary of me. Like they knew I was dangerous. Like they knew I could take them out with a flick of my wrist. "We just wanted to know if you would like to hang out with us? Go to the mall or something?"

"That's not really my thing." I replied back, trying to stay aloof. I wanted them gone. They didn't take the hint.

"Well, we could always go to the movies. Everyone likes that, right?" Tammy said.

"Yeah," Carly replied. "There has to be at least one movie you want to see."

I tried not to roll my eyes at their meager attempts to befriend me. It would be quite amusing, if they didn't annoy me so much.

"I already have plans, and they don't include going to the movies." I said, as I walked away. They followed.

"Will you at least tell us how to say your name? No one around here has a name like that. We really just want to get to know more about you." Of course, the leader, Samantha. Always the outspoken one, she just had to push it.

"My name is Avalonia and I am not from around here. That is all anyone needs to know."

I walked away as fast as I could without drawing attention. I just couldn't understand why they wanted to talk to, and get to know, me. I was the wallflower. The Plain Jane. They, themselves, were not very popular, but why did they notice me? I always did my best to go unnoticed. What had I done differently this time?

Chapter 7

Over the next few weeks, Samantha, Carly, and Tammy persisted. Asking me, everyday, to do one activity or another. It was dangerous, but I finally gave in.

It was a Friday night that I decided to go to the movies with them. For one: to get them to quit asking me, and two: because I was crazy bored.

Since I had to move schools every year, Michael could no longer come with me. He had obligations to the Council that could only be fulfilled in Astoria. It was decided that I would stay by myself from then on. I had been on my own since I turned fifteen. He would help me get settled in and would come to check on me once a month. Therefore, I had ran out of things to do by myself.

I had made sure to feed before I left. Being only half-vampire meant that I did not need to feed on blood as much as a full vampire: once a week, compared to everyday. But, even though I was only half-werewolf, I ate all the time, and large meals, at that. I could eat as much as a full grown, full blooded werewolf.

I met the girls right outside of the theater, at exactly 8 p.m. The movie started at 8:15. They were freaking out. Apparently, it is customary to get there at least half an hour early, to get the best seats.

Samantha was freaking out the most of all. "We are never going to get good seats, now! All the kids from school are already in there!"

Me being me, I plainly said, "You could have went in without me."

They all simultaneously gasped. I raised my eyebrows in question.

Tammy replied, "You never go in without all of your friends. What if something happened to them?"

That idea seemed absurd to me, but I could tell she was completely serious. I always forgot how weak humans are.

After them fretting, for the entire time it took us to get tickets, snacks, and seats, we finally got to watch the movie and I, finally, got some quiet. At least for awhile.

Once the movie was over, we went across the road to eat at The Diner, this little town's only fast food place. Cliché name, but they had great food. I hadn't eaten in hours and I was starving. I tried to order light, but, even then, I still got way more than the other girls.

"So, Avalonia..." Tammy started.

"Why did you move to our town?" Carly asked, while sharing a look with the other two.

"I just wanted to try out a new school. I didn't like my old one very much." I replied. Staring at anything but them. I wasn't used to situations like that.

"Your parents just let you? MIne wouldn't even let me go to school a town over. How far away from your old school are you?" Samantha enquired.

"My parents thought it would be best for me to be out on my own. I am 18. So, it really isn't up to them anymore. And my old school is about 6 hours from here." I decided answering them would be the best option. Maybe after tonight their curiosity would be filled and they would leave me alone. I could keep my secret easier that way.

As the night progressed, they asked me a lot of questions. Nothing very deep, though. It was like they really were trying to get me to be their friend, to open up, and get comfortable with them. Which, of course, set me on edge and made me want to leave town, but, at the same time, I felt wanted. Which is something I hadn't felt in a very long time.

Chapter 8

That night, on the way home, after leaving the girls at The Diner, I heard screams. My hybrid grew excited. So, of course, I had to check it out. The girls who were trying to become my friends were up against a wall. A gang of seven men was standing over them. They were advancing and the girls were scared, begging to be let go. I couldn't handle it. Their cries were too much. I began to *change*. My hybrid was enjoying the fear.

It was dark in the alley. There was a slim chance of me being seen, so I knew I needed to do something. Something that would keep both my human, and hybrid selves satisfied. The guys moved closer and, like that, my mind was made up.

I moved silently. Calling on all of my vampire abilities, I crossed the alley. Before the guys could reach their intended victims, they were down. I was able to control myself enough to only attack them, stopping short of killing. Now they were the ones crying in fear. Both sides of my hybrid felt complete. Awake. Happy. Fulfilled. Something I had not felt in a very long time! I was so distracted by that feeling, I almost let the girls see my face, which, up until then, was hidden in shadow. What I didn't think about them noticing was my shoes, and notice they did.

The next Monday, at school, the girls kept their distance. In a way, I was glad. No more having to constantly watch what I say and how I act, all the time. No more constantly keeping myself from *changing* and tearing them apart when they annoyed me. But, then again, I had gotten used to the constant buzzing of their chatter. I actually missed it.

The day passed in a blur. I was leaving school when they approached. They seemed wary. Scared. All of them.

"We just wanted to check on you." Samantha stated, meekly, which wasn't like her, at all. "We had some trouble on the way home from the movies and wanted to make sure you didn't. We didn't have your number or anything."

"I am fine. I went straight home after The Diner. Are you sure you guys are okay? What happened?" I asked, even though I already knew. I just hoped they didn't know it was me who saved them. But, how could they?

"Yeah, we are fine. Just a little shaken up. Someone saved us. We don't know who it was, all we saw were the shoes." Tammy said.

"They looked exactly like the ones you were wearing that night." Carly mumbled, thinking I couldn't hear. Tammy, who was close enough to hear her, elbowed her in the side.

That is when I knew they suspected something. What they thought was beyond me, but I knew I couldn't stay here much longer. I had to make sure my secret stayed safe.

"That is crazy. How can someone just come in and save you without you seeing them?" I asked.

"It was dark... We don't know how. They had to be crazy strong... And fast... There were seven guys! Who can take that many people out in just a few seconds?!" Samantha cried. Both girls grabbed and hugged her.

Carly said, "It had to of been a supernatural." My heart skipped a beat, my hands got clammy. Tammy and Samantha both looked at her like she had said something taboo. "You know, it could have been one of them, that snuck into our lands."

Both of the other girls looked at one another and started laughing. At least, for now, they don't believe her. But, what happens when the police report comes back and shows signs that it was a wolf attack? Then they will believe. Then they will piece it together. Then they will know.

Chapter 9

I went home and began packing, that night. I knew I had to leave. I couldn't take the chance in staying. They would find out. I had two options; leave, and destroy the report before I left, or kill them. I chose the first option.

That is the night it started to rain. I could hear it softly hitting the roof as I packed. I would make a letter for the girls. Some lame excuse about being called home. Needing to be there as soon as I could. I had it all planned, that is, until my doorbell rang.

I answered the door with an air of caution. No one knew where I lived. The only one who even had my address was the school, and I don't think the principal would just hand out that information. Apparently someone had, because standing in front of me was Samantha, Tammy, and Carly.

I just stared at them and they back at me. I cleared my throat.

"How did you find me?" I asked, while raising my eyebrows.

"Uhhhhm..." Samantha started, "We broke into the school office and got your address. The police stopped by with the report today." The air hung thick with tension.

"Aaannnddd?" I inquired. Slightly freaking out. I did not want to have to kill them. My hybrid, on the other hand, was giddy with anticipation.

Carly and Tammy looked at each other, then to Samantha. Carly turned back to me, then said, "We know it was you. "

"What are you talking about?" I asked, trying to act puzzled. I was freaking out inside. My hybrid was getting more excited by the minute.

Tammy gulped, then said, "They found wolf bites all over the bodies. Carly said it had to have been supernatural. We just laughed at her. But... She was right. It was you. We pieced it together. The shoes... The bites..." She started shaking.

"You are a werewolf!" Samantha finished. She was shaking slightly, herself, but, when I looked at her, she stood up straighter. Trying to act like she wasn't scared.

That was it, the words that I had waited all my life to hear and the words that I had so dreaded. Now, I had no choice. My human took a figurative step back in my mind. My hybrid came forward.

"Why don't you come in, so I can explain everything to you?" **They** asked. "I really like you guys and would like to keep you as friends. Please!" **They** practically begged.

The girls looked at each other, having a silent argument, then back at me. "Alright." They said in unison.

As I shut the door behind me, I thanked my parents for renting a house so secluded. My hybrid would get **their** way, today.

Just over the sounds of rain and thunder, the screams began. Being the monster that I so hated, I lavished in the moment. My human side cringed as they begged and pleaded for their lives. During this, I noticed Samantha was wearing a red shirt. Oh wait, it was white.

Maybe the next town will be different. Maybe next time no one will die.

Chapter 10

After the events in the last town, my parents and the Council decided it would be best for me to return home. To finally return to my family, pack, and coven. I had learned everything that I was going to in the Human Lands, anyway.

I had not seen my parents since I left home almost eleven years ago. I was nervous. Would they even recognize me? Would they still love me after the horrible things that I did to those girls? These were just some of the questions running through my head. None of which would have mattered had I known that not only had my parents heard of what I had done, so had the entire pack and coven.

Upon my return, everyone was there. Hundreds of people were standing before me. They all looked wary. My parents being the only exception. That is how my fears were abated and realized, at the same time. I may have came home to my parents, but the pack and coven no longer considered me family. I was an outsider. Something that they did not know how to control.

As I stepped out of the car, my mother rushed forward and hugged me.

" Oh, my baby!" She cried, as she desperately hung on to me.

"Let me have a chance to hug my daughter." My father said, laughing, as he gently pulled me out of my mother's arms. "Welcome home, Avalonia." He said joyfully.

"It is great to be home." I said, trying to sound convincing. I did not want my worries to show through.

My father turned to the pack and coven. "Welcome home, Avalonia!" My father shouted.

The pack replied in shouts and cheers of welcome, but, in their eyes, I could still see the doubt. I would have to work hard to win my pack and coven back. I would have to prove to them that I could control the monster. That I could, and would, be safe to have in their family.

That night, my parents set up an elaborate party. Everyone was there. The house looked amazing. There were lights strung from every tree and beautiful hanging-lanterns strung around the gazebo. It looked magical.

My parents were over the moon. For the past eleven years, they had done anything and everything to keep their minds off of my absence. It is very unusual for wolves or vampires to be away from their young. A few times, they considered giving up their positions so I could come home. I would not allow it. They both worked hard to gain those positions and I would not allow them to throw that away for me. Throughout the night, they never strayed far from my side. I always had one, or the other, close at hand. After years alone, it felt weird, but, at the same time, I felt safe. Loved.

About an hour after it started, my parents brought a few people over for me to meet.

"Avalonia, do you remember Alice, Lydia, and Tina?" My mother asked.

"Yes," I bluntly replied, startled. Not really knowing why they were asking. I had not noticed the girls standing next to them. My thoughts had been wandering.

"Well, since you girls were such great friends as children, we thought you may enjoy getting to know each other, now." My mother stated, looking hopeful.

I looked at the girls, they looked terrified. They were literally shaking. I remembered having the best of times with them, as a child. We always were getting into some sort of trouble. I really wanted to try and be friends with them. I mean it would be safe. They were werewolves. They already knew my secret and could protect themselves from me if need be. But, I couldn't see myself forcing them. I knew they did not want anything to do with me, so I said...

"I don't think it is such a good idea. We all know what happened the last time." My parent's faces fell.

The girls were visibly relieved. I could tell they were all silently thanking me. My human side was happy that I actually did something nice. My wolf and vampire, not so much. **They** wanted the girls to be scared. **They** wanted everyone scared of me.

As the night progressed, my parents tried, multiple times, to get me to talk to people. Each time, I refused. I was on the verge of losing control. My wolf was feeding on the fear. Feasting. Everyone here was afraid of me, in some small way. **She** wanted out.

I told my parents that I needed to be excused. They asked no questions, which was a good thing. How was I supposed to tell them that their little girl was already fantasizing of tearing their pack apart? They would have to report me to the Council and that would kill them. I ran, as quickly as I could, to my room. I changed clothes and snuck out the back. I needed to get away. Away from the fear. That would be the only way to calm my wolf.

I spent hours in the woods. Just letting my wolf be free. I knew **she** wanted to hunt, but after my inner turmoil, earlier, I could not risk letting **her** fully in control. Because if **she** took full control, my vampire would take advantage. *She* was conniving. *She* would do anything for blood. I would not be able to control who, or what, was killed. It was too dangerous, this close to the pack and coven.

I fell asleep sometime in the early morning, after my wolf had finally calmed down. I awoke to people shouting my name. I followed the sounds of their footfalls. There were hundreds of wolves. All trying to catch my scent. Which was hard for them, since I had just gotten back and my scent was new to them. My father was standing in the middle of a huge clearing, the one I first *changed* in.

"Avalonia!" My father shouted again.

"I am here, Dad." I said.

He turned around. He looked ready to kill. "Where have you been all night?! " He shouted. "We were worried sick."

My wolf and vampire, who had been calm after my sleep, did not like this, at all. "I told you I needed to get away, last night." I spoke slowly, through gritted teeth. I was trying not to growl. My father was an Alpha and his wolf, like mine, did not like to be disrespected. I knew that if we both let our wolves out, one of us, if not both, would die.

He sighed, trying to calm down. "We didn't think you meant from us. What is going on? Are you not happy being home?" He asked. As he spoke, his tone went from angry, to worried, to sad.

I closed my eyes and breathed deeply. I, too, needed to calm down. "I have been alone for a very long time. The party was just too much, too soon." I stated, not really lying or telling the full truth.

His face calmed down. "I am so sorry. We didn't think of that." He said. "We just wanted to show off our daughter. We missed you."

My human side felt bad. I was so worried about myself that I had forgotten about them.

"I am sorry, too." I stated. That seemed to be enough for him, as he quickly pulled me into a hug.

After we made it home, my mother yelled at me, for what seemed like hours. My vampire was scared, a first for the vampiric side of my hybrid, but not for me. I was terrified. My mother was a much older vampire than *her*. My werewolf, though, hated it, but knew that, with my vampire scared, **we** would never let **her** change and attack.

Chapter 11

Over the next few months, I was able to keep myselves in check. It was by no means easy being around such dominating personalities like werewolves and vampires, but, in a way, it was good. My monsters knew if **they** changed and attacked, that the pack and coven would attack, too, as a whole. Therefore, **they** stayed in check. Which made it easier on my human side.

One downside was, I was getting complacent. My human had grown used to the constant battling and, without it, grew weaker. I did not realize it, at the time, but I would find out, soon.

The night of my nineteenth birthday came, and with it a huge party. In werewolf culture the nineteenth birthday was very important, it is the day that you are finally able to sense your mate.

Like all nineteenth birthdays before mine, the party was held at the clearing that I *changed* in. I knew it had to happen, but I hated that place. That was the place where I became a monster. The place that changed my life forever.

My mother had a lavish gown made for me. It was red silk, the color of blood, the sign of the Vampires. My father had a sash made for me, black with a bright gold wolf emblazoned on it: the symbol for the Alpha family in our pack. Together the garments were lovely. I allowed myself a moment to enjoy them before I had to head into the chaos. I could hear the crowd from my bedroom window. Packs and covens from all over came to celebrate and see who would be my mate. If my mate even happened to be here.

"The Council has just arrived." My father stated, as he walked into the room.

My heart began to race. I had avoided them for the previous few months, but now I had to face the very people who I still believed, after all this time, wanted me dead. The very people who had experimented on me. The very people who I felt were trying to create a new army of hybrids. I could feel my hybrid start to surface, but I was able to push **them** down.

"Let's go." My mother said, as she looked at me, worriedly.

"I will be fine, Mom." I whispered, trying to reassure us both.

She smiled lovingly at me, as we started down the stairs.

As we headed toward the clearing, the music and voices got louder. It was crazy. I had never been around this many people at once. I was beginning to hyperventilate. My mother grabbed my hand to calm me down.

It was almost time. My father walked to the stage. I gathered all my courage and strength, and put on a brave face.

"May I have your attention, everyone!" He said in his booming Alpha voice. It got quiet instantly. "As you all know, we are here to celebrate my daughter Avalonia's nineteenth birthday." Cheers erupted. He raised his hand. "It is almost midnight. Which means, she will officially be nineteen and be able to sense her mate, if he is here, and, if you are her mate, you will be able to sense her. So, I just want to say that, any mate must see me first. I am her father. I must approve!" He boomed. All that could be heard was "Yes, Alpha." from our pack, coven, and those who were guests.

The countdown began. 10...My heart rate spiked... 9...My mouth was dry... 8...My hands clammy... 7...I began to shake... 6...I didn't want a mate right now... 5...Would he want me... 4...I was terrified of rejection... 3...I grabbed my mother's hand once more... 2...So close... 1...And... Nothing. No pull. No sense of my mate. I was relieved. Then worried. Was I broken? Could I just not sense him? Would he sense me and come to me? Was he even here? All these questions, and more, raced through my mind as everyone waited. One minute passed. Then five. Time passed so slowly, with no one making a sound. It was excruciating.

Finally, my father cleared his throat. "Well, then..." He said. "Let's kick this party off!"

My mother looked slightly disappointed, but quickly regained her composure. She turned, smiled brightly at me, and gave my hand a squeeze.

Music started blaring. It took a few minutes, but people finally stopped staring and moved on. It wasn't uncommon for people to not find their mate, but I assume that they thought, since I was a hybrid, I would have double the chance of finding my mate right away. I was in no big rush, though. I had enough to deal with at that moment. My hybrid was more than enough for me to handle.

I was dancing with my father, trying to take my mind off of the fact that I hadn't found my mate. I was scared to find him, but, now that I hadn't, I was afraid I never would. My father spun me around the dance floor and I laughed. He was a nice distraction. Once the song was over, I went to grab some punch.

The party was actually going great, despite the location. I was having a great time, but I let myself forget, for a moment, that I always needed to stay on guard. That I always needed to be ready to prevent *the change.*

All at once, I felt it. **They** both surged forward. Coming forward enough to lock me in my own mind. I watched my reflection in the punch bowl, waiting for the *change,* but the only thing that changed was my eye color. My once green eyes were now black. No one seemed to notice. **They** smiled wickedly.

They wanted to be free and free **they** were. There was nothing I could do, locked inside. I was trapped in my own mind. How could I let this happen? I had to find a way to escape.

I couldn't understand why **they** were not attacking, but **they** had become smarter than that. **They** knew to attack here would be a death sentence. **They** needed to go somewhere where **they** could hunt, but not get killed.

They spotted my mother and made **their** way to her. My vampire spoke in her easy voice. Trying to perfectly imitate me.

"We..." *She* cleared her throat."I mean, *I* am tired. *I* wish to go lie down."

They were smart enough to hide my eyes in shadow. My mother had not noticed the difference. I was screaming at her from inside my mind. Begging her to help me. My wolf was silently laughing at me. **They** knew my mother could not hear me.

She must have assumed that the pressure of not finding my mate was too much for me, because she agreed almost instantly. "Okay, darling. Go get you some rest. The party is almost over, anyway." She said adoringly.

They were elated. **They** began to walk back toward the house. Once out of sight, **they** made a break for it. Running as fast as my vampire could go. Running away from the place that I was just starting to consider, once again, as home.

We were almost at the border when **they** looked back laughing. I could faintly see the lights from the party. I made a vow. I would get my body back and I would conquer these monsters, once and for all.

Chapter 12

Later on I learned what was happening in the pack and coven, while I was gone.

It took them a day to realize that I was gone. They wanted to give me space. They assumed that the party was too much for me and that I wanted to be alone. The night after the party my mother came to check on me. When I didn't answer my door, or her calls, she came into my room. It was empty, of course. She searched the room. Checking the closet, the bathroom, and even under the bed. When she couldn't find me, and saw no sign that I had came back there the previous night, she yelled for my father.

She was crying hysterically when my father arrived. It took him a while to calm her down enough to figure out what was wrong. When he finally got it out of her, he went on a rampage. He tore apart my room. His rage got the better of him. Unable to search gently like my mother, everything was ruined. My mother finally calmed him enough so that he could *change* back to human form. After which, he went outside and addressed everyone who had stayed after my party. That included; my pack and coven, and the various packs and covens who did not wish to make the long journeys home so soon after the party.

"Where is my daughter?" My father bellowed, shaking from the strain of not *changing* and tearing everything apart until he found me. My mother was not much better. She had moved past being scared and sad, that I was gone, her usually calm demeanor had turned furious. Her fangs were out. Eyes turned black as night.

My father's question was returned only by blank stares. No one said a word. This made him even more furious. How could his daughter just disappear? He had guards checking the borders constantly. He fully *shifted* and began to run. My mother was not far behind. They made it to the border in no time. My father tried to catch a scent of me all along the border. He couldn't find one. Even though he had become re-familiar with my scent, the scents from all of the wolves who patrolled the borders had covered mine.

The Alphas of the other packs stepped forward and *changed* back to their human forms. SIgnalling my father to *change,* as well. They all looked at each other.

Alpha Carson, whose pack was closest to ours, spoke first. "I give you permission to search my lands for your daughter." He said, while looking my father in the eye, as is customary. All Alphas had to give permission for anyone to enter their lands. If you did not have permission, the Alpha had the right to kill you. All of the other Alphas soon followed suit.

"Thank you, all. I will set up teams of my men. If you would not mind, could some of yours help them look?" My father addressed all the Alphas.

They all said "Yes".

After they returned to the pack house, my mother went in search of the coven. My father began to divide his men into groups. It took him a few hours to organize. Our pack was large. Over one thousand people. He had to make sure that all of the groups were evenly matched. They all needed to have great trackers and warriors. My father did not know if someone had taken me, so they needed to be prepared.

My mother, meanwhile, had been talking to her coven. She wanted them to help search for me. They could not smell me as strongly as the wolves but they could search more ground. Most of the coven did not want to go with the wolves. They may live on packlands, but they were still stuck in their old ways. They still believed that wolves were the enemy. They were only here because their Súmaire was, unfortunately, mated to one. Furthermore, these same vampires wanted nothing to do with me. I was half wolf, which, to them, meant that I was half-enemy.

The coven was split fifty/fifty, on this front. The younger vampires were more open to the wolves. They also liked me. I was the daughter of their Súmaire. Therefore, I was to be respected, so as not to disrespect her.

It took my mother much time and effort, but she was finally able to convince everyone to help. The older vampires were to go out on their own and search, after my mother got permission from all the alphas. The younger ones would go along with the wolves.

The other covens had agreed to help, right away. They had been patiently waiting outside for my mother. Once she finally got her coven to agree to help, they headed back toward my father and the packs.

The wolves, like the vampires, still felt that the other species were their enemies. Unlike the coven, the pack had more of an eighty/twenty split. The ones who liked the vampires were the children and some young adults. They had grown up with the coven, so they did not see them as a threat.

The covens arrived just as the wolves were setting out on their journeys. Some wolves could be heard saying "What are they doing here?" "For all we know, they did something to her." "If they are going, I am not." And so on. The vampires did not appreciate being disrespected in this way. All of them had their fangs out, preparing for a fight. Even the ones who liked the wolves.

My mother stepped through them, to the front of all the vampires. My father met her in the middle. Werewolf hearing is not as good as vampire hearing, so he did not hear all the remarks. My mother had, though, and she was furious.

"You need to keep your wolves in check!" She hissed at my father. He may be her mate, but she would not let anyone disrespect her coven.

My father looked bewildered. "I don't know what you mean." He said, while looking around at them all. "What have they done?"

She told him what they had said. As she did, the pack could tell their Alpha was getting madder by the second. They all began to inch backwards. Even some of the other packs began to, also.

"What is the meaning of all this? Even after all this time, you do not trust her coven enough to not speak out of turn to them! You dare say all these things to my mate's coven!" He yelled, staring them all down.

One brave wolf stepped forward, he was new to the pack, "Vampires have been our enemy for hundreds of years. Why should we have to bear their presence because you have the unfortunate luck to be mated to one?" He said. He had a smirk on his face, which was soon erased. As soon as he finished talking, my father attacked. He was lucky to survive. My mother pulled my father off of him.

"We do not have time for this!" She whispered, trying to calm him down.

My father *shifted* back. "You're right." He said, looking at her. He then addressed the packs. "We may have been enemies before, but, the moment I met Melovanin, we became a family. I know you do not like each other, and you probably never will, but we need to band together to find Avalonia. She is your future Luna." He said to the pack. "And your future Súmaire." to the coven. "You should all want her back. She is the future of us all. You need to work together to ensure that future. Now, let us go and find her!" He shouted, as he *changed* into his wolf.

He charged out through all the packs. My mother right by his side. The packs and covens looked at each other. They may hate and distrust each other, but they had to put that aside, at least for today. They soon followed. Each headed to their designated areas to search.

The search parties stayed out for a week. Each one slowly losing members as they gave up hope. My parents were the last two out searching. They did not want to give up, but knew they must, for the survival of the pack and coven. They reluctantly went home.

There had been turmoil between the pack and coven since the day the search began. There had been fights breaking out nightly. The wolves words had even turned the younger vampires against them. My parents were the only thing holding the pack and coven together. If they were not there, the coven and pack would tear each other apart.

Once they returned from the search, my parents were able to stop the fights. But the peace didn't last long. Two weeks after they returned, a fight between the guard wolves and some of the men in the coven broke out. My parents arrived just in time to prevent someone from dying. A few from both coven and pack landed in the hospital.

That is when my mother realized, no matter how much she loved her coven, she would have to step down as Súmaire. That way the coven could leave and return to the Vampire Lands. Later that night, she went and spoke to them.

"This has gone too far. We have lived peacefully for twenty-nine years, and now, both the pack and you have decided it can't be done any more. I can not allow this turmoil to go on." She closed her eyes and breathed deeply, trying to gather her courage. "I can not leave this pack. My mate is here. My home is here, now, but you all can." The coven began to protest. She raised her hand and they quieted. "I know that you do not wish to leave me. I have been your Súmaire for a very long time, but due to the events of the past few weeks, it is time for me to step down, and for you to elect a new Súmaire. You will be able to return to the Vampire Lands and live peacefully." She said, while trying to hide the fact that she was crying.

Mavis, the oldest vampire, after my mother, spoke up. "We do not wish to leave you, but we understand where you are coming from. I believe I speak for everyone..." He said while looking around at the room. The coven all subtly nodded. "...when I say that we will not accept your resignation."

My mother began to interrupt. "But..."

Mavis continued "We will not accept your resignation, but we will elect a temporary Súmaire, or Súmaise, and return to the Vampire Lands. It will be best for all. We will be safe and happy," He smiled at my mother. "And you will continue to be our Súmaire. We would not have anyone else as our Súmaire."

My mother began to bawl. His words were the nicest thing anyone, other than her mate, had ever said to her. "I accept your proposal." She said through her tears. "I would like to nominate you, Mavis, to be the temporary Súmaise. Does everyone agree?"

The coven cheered. They had come to a decision that worked for everyone. It was not, by any means, the best, but it was what needed to be done.

That night, my mother stayed with the coven and helped them pack. They stayed up all night, chatting and packing. The next morning, my mother saw the coven off. They had a long way to travel before they reached the Vampire Lands and their new home.

My father was awoken by the sounds of my mother crying. She did not tell him of her plan until after she had already done it. My father held her as she cried. He knew it was hard for her to have her coven leave, but he knew that she was just doing what was best for them. He just had to keep reminding her of that.

Over the next few months, the pack lived in peace. Even though my mother was a vampire, the pack appreciated her having the coven leave. They began to see her as more than just the Alpha's mate. She was finally their Luna.

My mother received word, a week after the coven left, that they were safe. The coven didn't like to use cell phones. They were stuck in the old ways, rarely even using landline phones. The older vampires hated cars. They could run just as fast as them. So, why bother. Over the months, she continued to receive weekly reports. She was happy that her coven was safe and happy. Even if she missed them deeply.

My parents didn't give up the search. Every day a group of wolves was sent out to search our lands and the surrounding packlands. They did not give up hope that I would return.

Chapter 13

It had been a month since **they** had taken over. I was miserable. **They** had been gorging **themselves** on anything, and anyone, **they** could find. I seemed to be slowly gaining my strength back. For the most part, **they** ignored me, but always made sure I was safely tucked into my "cage". My "cage" was just the darkest reaches of my mind. The spot in the back of my mind where all of my fears and doubts rested.

They had found a spot in the mountains where **they** knew **we** wouldn't be found. For the first few weeks **we** ran. **They** ran as far and as fast as **they** could. My pack came very close to finding **us**, on a few occasions. In a way, I wanted them to. Maybe then they would notice that I wasn't myself. That **they** had taken over. Maybe then they could help, but **they** somehow always managed to elude them. Maybe that was for the best. I didn't want to hurt anyone in my pack.

I had been forming a plan for the past few weeks. I would need to gain as much strength as possible. My human needed to be stronger than it ever had before. Once at full capacity, I would surge forward and do to **them** what **they** had done to me. I would cage the monsters. I would finally be free!

Being trapped inside was horrible. It was taking a toll. I had to remind myself why I was doing this. Even though I had been away from my parents, pack, and coven for so long, I still considered them family. They gave me a reason to live. I couldn't give up.

I was next in line to be leader of the pack and coven. I had to make sure that I would either be a great leader or be there to find someone who would. I did not know how my plan would affect my supernatural sides. Would I even still be considered a supernatural if I locked them inside? Would **they** even still exist if I kept **them** locked away for too long?

It was a chance that I was willing to take. These monsters inside me needed to be contained and controlled. I could no longer rely on others to help me, to be there to clean up my messes. I was responsible. It was something I should have realized a long time ago.

As I finally came to this realization, my strength started to increase on a daily basis. I was finally able to see my human as something other than weak. I was strong and I would prove it.

Over the next few months, I played the perfect prisoner. **They** were beginning to grow complacent with me. **They** thought I had given up. **They** thought **they** were finally free. I let **them** believe it.

They relished in being free. **They** had been hunting every night since **they** had taken over. Blood and meat was all my diet consisted of. Deer had become my wolf's favorite meal.

Chapter 14

It started out as an ordinary day trapped inside, but I soon realized something was different. **They** seemed on edge. I could tell something was coming. I was right. A human had made his way onto our lands. **They** were growing wild in anticipation. He was drawing closer. **They** were salivating. That is when I knew I had to strike. I closed my eyes and used all of my strength. I surged forward!

I only went forward enough to enter the center of my mind. I wanted to draw **them** out of the control center. I needed them out if I was going to take control back.

The center planes of my mind looked like a forest. My favorite place. I knew the trees were not really there, but they gave me comfort. They gave me strength.

At first **they** didn't notice that I had moved. **They** were distracted by thoughts of how it was such great luck the human had come upon us. It took a moment, but when **they** did realize, **they** were furious.

My wolf growled. My vampire let out an unearthly scream. **They** both dove backward into my mind and, thankfully, out of the control center.

My body went slack. No one was in control. From the outside, I probably looked like a zombie. I could only hope this battle didn't last long. I needed to take control before something happened to my body or it completely shut down and I died.

I was terrified, but I knew I had to do this. Not only for me, or this human, but for my family. I ran straight at **them**.

They had fangs and claws. I had no weapon but my wits. I had to think fast.

I stopped just short of **them**, which startled **them**. So **they** stopped, as well. **They** looked at me, puzzled. I was just happy that it had worked. I was hoping the rest of my plan would, also. I looked at my wolf and said...

"Are you not sick of all the blood? I know you prefer your meat cooked. I mean, yeah, blood is good, some of the time, but who wants to eat it all of the time?"

My wolf just looked puzzled. **She** couldn't figure out what I was trying to do. I knew, from my father and other pack members, that werewolves preferred their meat cooked. They like raw meat on occasion, but cooked meat tasted better to them. My wolf had no choice, though. Since **they** both were in the foreground of my mind, **she** had to eat raw, so my vampire could get blood. When **they** trapped me **they** took away their option to eat separately.

My vampire looked at my wolf. Waiting for her to speak. Since **she** didn't, I turned to my vampire.

"Are you not sick of all the meat? Does it not disgust you to have all that solid food? Wouldn't you much rather just have the blood?"

She turned **her** head to the side. **She** was pondering what I said. My vampire had always had a deep, psychological hate for meat, even though our body could digest it just fine. So, I knew, with **her** being constantly forward, that **she** was getting sick from it. I was hoping my vampire's base need for survival would win, over **her** intellect.

My wolf was looking at *her*. **She** could tell my vampire was thinking about it, and I could tell, so was **she**. **They** hated each other's diets. It was also taking a toll on my body. Which, I knew **they** felt. My plan was simple. I would target them both, try to get one to turn on the other. My vampire was the most likely to turn on my wolf. Vampires are less loyal. They care more about their own survival than anything else.

I watched my vampire closely. I could see it in *her* eyes when *she* had made *her* decision. A sly smirk made its way onto *her* face.

My wolf noticed, right after I did. I could feel the betrayal rolling off **her** in waves. **She** lunged. My vampire was fast enough to get out of the way. The battle began. All I could see were the two beings scratching, biting, and clawing. **They** were everywhere.

I knew I would only have a few minutes before one of them killed the other. Then, whoever was left, **their** attention would turn to me. I had to find a way past. **They** were so focused on each other that **they** had forgotten about me. **They** rolled right next to me. I saw my chance. I began to run as fast as I could, toward the light.

I could hear **them** behind me. **They** had finally realized what I had done. I just kept telling myself "It is only a little further. You can do it." My vampire was fast. I was lucky that I was able to get a head start. I was so close. I could hear her right behind me. I was right in front of the light. I could feel her. She was so close. I reached out my hand and hoped, beyond hope, that I was close enough.

I kept my eyes closed and prayed that it had worked. That I had finally trapped **them**. Finally conquered **them**. I opened my eyes to see a human man staring at me. I did it!

I could hear **them** inside, but not as loud as before. I had succeeded in pushing **them** back and locking **them** in. I had won! I began to smile uncontrollably. I was ecstatic.

This human probably thought I was insane. Especially, since I ran and hugged him. I was in desperate need to feel something real.

"I am so sorry." I began. "I have been lost here, for what seems like forever." I said. Not really lying, since I was lost, in my own mind.

He stared for a moment longer, then said,"It is okay. My name is Damian. I can try to help you find your way out, if you like."

Damian was a handsome man. He had black hair, bright blue eyes, and a strong physique. I was instantly attracted to him.

"Thank you, so much," I said. " My name is Avalonia. I am from the south of here. The Wolf Lands that are closest to the human border."

He looked amazed. "No wonder you are lost." He said. "We are on the opposite side of your lands. Just inside The Witchlands."

My mouth made an "o" shape. I knew **they** had taken me far, but I did not realize how far.

My face made him laugh. I composed myself and asked. "What is a human doing in The Witchlands?"

Each species had their own scent. It was one way for us to tell what species they were. That is how I knew he was a human. His scent remained in my nose even though my hybrid had been locked away.

He looked like he didn't know whether to say, or not.

"If you can't tell me, it is fine. It is just unusual." I sputtered out.

"My grandmother is a witch." He said. "We should get going. It will be getting dark soon."

I relished in the moment of freedom that I felt. I could finally be around someone and not want to kill them. I felt amazing, but, at the same time, sad. Even though **they** were horrible. I felt like I was missing a piece of me. But, I knew that I would have to learn to live with it, because, after living my entire life in fear, I was finally free!

Part III

Chapter 15

It took Damian and me almost three months to reach my father's land. It was safer for a human to travel by foot through the Wolf Lands, since they were not supposed to be there, and, since my hybrid had ran all the way to the Witchlands, we had no choice but to walk.

During this time we grew closer. We spent hours by the fire, every night, talking. I was beginning to fall for him, but whether or not he was my mate, I couldn't tell. The two parts of me who could tell were locked up in the darkest reaches of my mind. I had made the decision not to listen to **them**. So, I guess I would never know, but, to me, it didn't matter. Those three months were the happiest months that I could remember since my *change*.

Though I was content during my waking hours, my dreams were haunted by nightmares. Nightmares of what I had done to the girls that I had called friends. Many nights Damian would wake me. I would thrash around in my nightmarish state and he was afraid that I would hurt myself. I didn't tell him what they were about and he never asked. He just held me and let me cry.

It was on the last night of our journey that I decided to tell Damian my story. I guess I just felt like he needed to know. I wanted him to know who I truly was. I wanted to give him the chance to leave before we reached my father's land.

I expected him to scorn me. I expected him to just get up and walk away. To yell. Do anything, except what he did. He looked across the fire and straight into my eyes. He looked as if he was going to speak, then stopped. All of the fear and worry that I felt must have been showing on my face. He got up, but he didn't leave like I had expected, instead, he kept eye contact with me and walked toward me. Then he hugged me. He started to push me away and I feared then he would leave, but he surprised me once again. He grabbed my face and looked into my eyes and, before I had a chance to react, he kissed me. It only lasted a moment, but it was then that I knew I loved him. He was the one. Even if he wasn't my "mate".

After that night he knew what my nightmares were about.

We entered into my father's land early in the day, on the last day of July. It was a beautiful morning. I knew we needed to be careful. I had no idea if my scent had changed since I locked **them** up or not. If the pack scouts did not recognize me, we could be killed on sight.

As I was thinking this, I felt a shift in the air. I pushed Damian behind me and closed my eyes. I expected an attack and without my hybrid I was unable to protect us. All I could do was brace myself for the impact. I heard growls. A wolf was standing in front of us. After a moment, more wolves joined the first. They had been drawn by the growls. One of the wolves took off in the opposite direction, toward the pack house. I could only hope that he was headed to get my father. I had to remain as quiet as possible during that time. If I even attempted to address the wolves, while trespassing and being accompanied by a human, they would kill without hesitation. It was only one of the many rules I had learned as a child.

Luckily, I was right. Within ten minutes the wolf returned, my father right behind him. My father began to *turn* human. I closed my eyes. I could feel his eyes burning a hole in my skin. Damian adjusted his position, trying to get between me and them. He wanted to protect me, even if it was from wolves.

"Avalonia?" I heard my father whisper.

I finally dared to look up. He was just staring at me, looking as if he had seen a ghost. I began to talk, when he held up a hand, silencing me. He turned to the wolves.

"Bring them both to the pack house. Bring her to my office. Treat them gently. I do not want to see a scratch on either of them." He said, as he turned and *changed* back into his wolf. He headed back toward the house.

A few moments later, we were on our way behind him. The wolves surrounded us, making sure we could not escape. I could feel the hate running off of Damian. I knew this would be tough on him. He was strong and brave for a human. Being trapped was not an ideal situation. He had no idea how this would turn out. For that matter, neither did I.

Once we reached the pack house, they separated us. That is when Damian began to fight. I knew it would not turn out good if he kept resisting them. I had to get him to stop before he got hurt.

"Damian, I will be okay. I will find you. I will get this taken care of. I promise." I told him.

He stopped resisting, almost immediately. He nodded his head as they dragged him away. I was led into the house and into my father's office. That was the first time I had ever felt fear when entering my father's office.

Chapter 16

When I entered his office, my father was sitting at his desk. His head was bowed. It looked as if he had a heavy weight on his shoulders.

"Alpha..." The wolf who brought me in began. I had never seen him before.

My father just raised his hand and waved him away. The wolf bowed and left.

It took my father an excruciatingly long five minutes to speak to me. During that time, I had a lot of thoughts running through my head. Mainly about how I was going to tell him what was truly going on with me and how I was going to save Damian.

"Avalonia, where have you been? Why did you leave? Do you know how worried we have been? Do you have any idea what your disappearance did to the pack and coven?" His voice raised with each question. I was shaking in fear. For once, my hybrid wasn't there to want to fight back. "Well, answer me!" He finally shouted. I began to cry.

His cold demeanor began to crack. Even if he was mad at me, his child was in pain and he could not stand to see it. He walked around the desk and hugged me.

He gave me a few moments then said, "Please. Tell me, Avalonia."

I gathered what little composure I could muster and began to tell my story.

"I left because I lost control. It had been happening for awhile..." I went on to tell him everything that had happened. When I finished his face looked stricken.

"How could we not have noticed? Why didn't you tell us?" He asked. As he looked me in the eyes, I could see the sadness in his.

"I was afraid. **They** were dangerous. I knew you would have to do something about it. I didn't want to be locked up again. Or, even worse, be killed. What will the Council do to me, now?" I asked him.

He sighed, then lowered his gaze to the floor. After a moment he looked up, then said, "Nothing, they will do nothing."

I didn't get a chance to ask him what he meant. He was up on his feet and headed to the door before I could say anything.

"Thomas, bring the human here. Unharmed." My father said. Then he turned and walked to his desk, looking for something. I knew there was no point in interrupting him. He had a one-track mind. He would never even hear me.

A few minutes later, as my father continued searching, Thomas brought Damian inside. Damian tried to come to me, but Thomas pulled him back.

"Alpha, here is the hhhumann." He practically growled out human. "Unharmed. Like you said."

"Thank you, Thomas. You may leave." My father said. He had finally found what he was looking for. A key. I did not know what it was for.

My father turned to Damian. "I assume my daughter has filled you in on her situation."

Damian looked at me, trying to see if I was okay with him telling my father. I nodded, then Damien looked back at my father and did the same.

"Very well, then. I need you to do something for me. I need you to take Avalonia into the Human Lands." He said, while handing Damian the key. "This is the key to our only car. I want you to take her to the furthest reaches of the Human Lands. She can never return here."

I began to protest. "But father..."

"You will do this, Avalonia. It is the only way to ensure the Council never finds out. No one here, besides me, knows who you are. No one will ever have to know you have returned." He said. Begging me with his eyes to understand why I needed to do this.

"Fine," I sighed. I knew a lost battle when I saw one. "I just want to say goodbye to Mother before I leave."

My father's face fell. "Your mother is not here. She is with the coven in the Vampire Lands."

I was surprised to hear that the coven had returned to the Vampire Lands after twenty-nine years.

"Why are they there? I know you said there were some problems between the pack and coven, but why did they leave? Did it truly get that bad? And why is mother with them?" I was firing question after question, until he placed a finger over my lips.

"Your mother is just there to check in on the coven. After you left, the pack and coven began blaming each other for your absence. It led to fights between the two. It was getting so bad that someone almost died. Your mother decided it would be best for the coven to return to their home, in the Vampire Lands." My father said.

I couldn't believe it. They had lived peacefully for twenty-nine years and all because I had disappeared they turned on each other.

"I know that look, Avalonia. It was not your fault. The pack and coven never truly got along. They are natural born enemies. It was only a matter of time before something like this happened." My father said.

It didn't make me feel much better but I did understand. It was hard for natural enemies to live together. My hybrid still had moments where the two sides fought.

"You need to go and pack some of your clothes, as quietly as possible. You can not let anyone see you. Meet us outside when you are finished." My father said, as he led Damian out the door.

It took me only ten minutes to pack my clothes. Most of them were still packed from my last time in the Human Lands. My hybrid had never cared about tidiness. Once packed, I met my father and Damian outside. Damian put my bags in the trunk, alongside his. I turned to my father and hugged him.

"I will miss you and mother." I said. It was the first time I had truly meant it. My hybrid didn't care when we left my parents the first time. All **they** cared about was getting away from the people who were controlling **them**. "Please, tell her."

"I will. " He said, he knew that I meant about everything. She needed to know. "Now, go. You must leave before anyone else wakes up."

I got in the car. Damian was already in the driver's seat. As soon as I got in, He looked over at me, grabbed my hand, and gave me a slight smile. Then he drove away from my father and pack. I watched my father through the rear view mirror, for as long as I could, before he disappeared.

Chapter 17

It took us three days to reach Damian's house. It was just outside of Astoria, which meant we had to be careful. I could not risk being seen. As far as we knew, the Council knew nothing of my troubles with my hybrid, but I knew that if they found me, they would return me to my pack. Then there would be questions. I had not come up with a reasonable lie that would pass the scrutiny of the Council. The witch on the Council was very good at detecting lies. It was believed that she would cast a spell over anyone she believed was being untruthful. After that, they could never tell a lie again.

Damian just needed to come to his house to gather up some of his things. I layed in the backseat of the car until he returned. While he was in the house, I thought about how I had changed his life over the last three months. I had completely turned his life around. Did he really want to be with me? Did he just feel sorry for me? Did he love me as much as I loved him? These questions, and more, were running through my head. I was just about to go in and talk to him, to risk being seen, when he returned.

"Where were you going?" He asked. The look on his face was pure terror. I wondered if that look meant that he did care.

"I was just adjusting. This backseat isn't as comfortable as it looks." I joked.

He laughed. "Okay. I thought for a minute you were leaving me. You had me scared."

"Why would I leave you? I would miss you." I said, while looking in his eyes.

The biggest smile I had ever seen made it's way onto his face. I smiled back. He got back into the car, and we were on our way, once more.

We travelled day and night, until we reached the opposite coast of the Human Lands. We came to a town that I had never been to before called Calista. It was beautiful. It had white sand beaches on one side and huge, glorious mountains on the other. It was my perfect paradise.

The first thing we did, when we arrived, was find a place to stay. We found the local realtor and used some cash that my father had stashed in the car to rent a place right on the ocean. It was a magnificent place. A two story cottage, with three bedrooms. It was the ideal place for us to stay.

After we got our living arrangements settled, we headed into town. It was customary in the Human Lands that when you first move to a new town you had to go to the local "hot spot". Every town had one. It was just a place, a restaurant, bar, or club, that everyone in town loved to go to. It gave the locals a chance to meet you and get to know you. I had never done it before. When my hybrid wasn't locked up, it was too dangerous, but I knew that I had to blend in here if I wanted to have a truly human life.

Throughout this entire journey, I did not once feel the urge to kill. It felt amazing. I could hear **them** screaming in the back of my mind. I was starting to get used to it. At the beginning, it was awful. **They** were so loud. I would get constant headaches. I had to train myself to tune **them** out. To push **them** further back into my mind. To the point that was more like a constant buzzing.

The local hot spot in Calista was a restaurant and bar. It was a cozy place. They had set it up to have a beachy feel. I loved it and could see why all the locals did, too.

As soon as we entered, everyone stopped what they were doing and turned to us. I began to back away. I was not used to this amount of attention. Damian grabbed my hand and gave me a half smile. He strode forward, straight to the hostess. "Table for two, please." Damian said, looking her straight in the eye.

She looked from him to me, then back. "Right this way." She said, as she led us to a table. "Here you go. You are not from around here, are you?" She asked Damian.

"No, my girlfriend and I just moved here. Can we get a couple of menus?" He said, daring her to say anything else. Meanwhile, I was speechless. Since when was I his girlfriend? I probably had a goofy grin on my face. I had been wanting to hear those words from him for a while. As soon as the waitress left, I asked him just that.

"Girlfriend, huh?" I said teasingly.

He scratched the back of his neck. He was looking everywhere but at me. He had a cute blush spreading across his cheeks. "She was looking at me like she wanted to eat me. I had to say something."

I started laughing. His face was priceless.

"It isn't funny." He mumbled, as she came back with our menus.

"Okay." I said trying to stifle my giggles. "I thought we were supposed to be nice to locals. Not be rude to the first one we meet." I joked.

He finally looked up into my eyes and he smiled. That was one of the best nights of my life, up to that point.

We spent hours there, mainly due to the fact that everyone there came and introduced themselves, which was customary in the Human Lands. I had never been able to be this social and I loved it. The people in this town were nice. They made us feel like we were home. I knew I was going to like it in that town. I would have been happy if I could have stayed there forever.

Chapter 18

Damian and I lived happily in Calista for three years. During that time, we grew closer.

The night Damian told me that he loved me started out like any other. We had ordered food from our favorite restaurant in town and we were watching a movie. I noticed, through it all, him staring at me. I looked his way and everytime he would look away. I grew confused and finally I couldn't take it any longer.

"Why do you keep looking at me like that?" I asked.

He looked at me sheepishly. He had not realized that I had noticed.

"I..." Damian said, then trailed off.

I gave him a moment to continue and when he didn't. I said. "Yes?" Urging him to continue.

He took a deep breath. "I love you!" He said, rushing out the words.

It took me a moment to comprehend what he said, but, when I realized, I smiled. I noticed him staring at me. Then it was my turn to look sheepish.

"I love you, too!" I said. Damian then leaned forward and kissed me.

He had helped me get through the regret of what I had done to those girls. He had helped me realize that I had no control over what **they** did, at that time. I would always regret it, but I couldn't change it. All I could do was work to ensure that nothing like that ever happened again.

I was actually able to make friends in Calista. I was becoming more confident and outgoing as time went on. My life was great. But that all changed the day that Michael showed up.

I was doing our weekly grocery shopping when I spotted him. I froze in place. How could he be here. This town was nowhere near Astoria. He was looking around for someone. I ducked behind a shelf, hoping he did not see me. I waited a few minutes, sat my stuff down, and turned the corner to leave. Instead, I ran straight into Michael. It was the worst of luck.

"I am so sorry, young lady. I wasn't watching where I was going." He said. Then he finally glanced down at me. His face paled. He had recognized me. "What are you doing here? You do not have permission to be here! The Council and your parents have been worried sick!"

There was no use in trying to deny that I knew him. I spent a lot of my childhood with this man. I was scrambling for what words to say, when a fire alarm went off. I took the chance and ran. I didn't get far. Damian was standing at the end of the aisle. He grabbed my arm and pulled me out the back door of the store. He had seen and overheard some of what was going on with Michael, and he knew we needed to leave.

We got into our car and drove off. No matter how safe we felt in this town, we always kept extra clothes and cash on hand, just in case. There would be no time to stop and grab our things. By now, Michael will have informed the Council and the Guard would be on their way. If some were not already here. We needed to hurry.

We traveled for days, getting as far away from that town as we could. I knew, by then, that almost all of the Guard would be out looking for me.

I could only hope that they didn't know about Damian.

Finally, we stopped at a little town on the beach. Michael knew my favorite spot was the mountains. I could only hope that is where he would think I would run to, that he would never suspect that I would go to the beach, the place where my journey in the Human Lands had started.

Instead of renting a house, like last time, Damian and I decided to just get a hotel room for a few nights. We did not feel secure enough to stay here for very long. We had no idea how far Michael had sent the Guard out to search.

We stayed only two days in that town. We heard rumors that the Guard was getting closer. It was uncommon for the Guard to travel outside of Astoria. So, it was a big deal for them to be seen there. We were hundreds of miles from Astoria. We had no idea which towns they were in, but assumed, since they were coming from the town we lived in, it would be best to stay on the path we were on. Heading back toward the Packlands.

We drove for days. We didn't plan on stopping but we saw signs of the Guard. They had placed a check point along the highway. Luckily, we were able to exit before we came to them. Our only option was to head north, toward Astoria. It was risky, but, also, the one place they would, hopefully, believe I was less likely to go. Our theory was that it would be safer.

We went to Damian's old house. He had decided not to sell it. He said he was keeping it for emergencies. I believe it was because that is where his parents raised him. Either way, I am glad he did. That house gave us shelter and as long as they didn't figure out who Damian was, we were safe from the Guard.

Damian's house was amazing. He had been paying a cleaning and gardening service to keep up his house while we were gone. It was two stories, had three bedrooms, and two bathrooms. I loved it. I hoped that we would be able to stay there for a very long time.

"I am going to call my grandmother. She may be able to help us." Damian said.

"Thank you. I could really use all the help I can get." I said, as I hugged him tightly. He kissed the top of my head and held me for a moment. I have no idea where I would be without him. He was my rock during those years.

As he went to call her, I looked around his house. I made my way into the master bedroom. It was gorgeous. The walls were blue and the furniture was brown. The linens were mixed blue and brown. It was my favorite combination. Damian and I had very similar tastes in our stylistic choices.

I fell asleep, in the master bedroom, while he was on the phone downstairs. He woke me up a few hours later.

"My grandmother said that we could stay in her house in the Witchlands, if we need to, but, it will be dangerous. We would either have to go through the Wolf Lands or through Astoria." He sighed. "I don't want to risk that if we don't have to. It would be best if we stayed here for a few days." He sat down beside me on the bed. I put my head on his shoulder and hugged him to me.

I trusted his judgment, so we decided to stay and get settled there. At least for a few days.

Chapter 19

We had settled in nicely, even getting a little comfortable, when the Guard made their way into town. We had no warning. We woke up one morning and they were there. Searching each and every house, forcefully. They had the right to enter anyone's house, even without permission.

We did not get a chance to run. By the time we realized they were in the town, they were busting down our door. They recognized me, right away. Apparently, Michael had a picture that he had circulated throughout the Guard.

They tried to grab me as soon as they saw me. Damian got in their way. They looked shocked. No one ever defied the Guard. They had permission to do whatever was necessary to get their job done. Damian was human. They were a mixed group of werewolves, vampires, and witches. He had no chance of defeating them.

I was having an internal debate. I could hear my hybrid selves for the first time in years. **They** were begging to be let out. **They** wanted to protect **their** mate.

"At least that question was answered." I thought to myself. Now, I just had to make the decision, let out the monster that haunted me throughout my life, to save the man I love, or keep them locked up, where I knew everyone would be safe from them. The choice was difficult, at first. I ran the risk of having my hybrid take over again. No matter how much **they** insisted **they** wouldn't, how could I ever trust **them**?

The Guard advanced on Damian. They grabbed his arms as he started to fight. He kept fighting, so they hit him over the head. With that, my mind was made up. Damian would know if **they** took over and would do something about it. After years of mental captivity, I allowed my hybrid to take control.

Once **they** came forward the battle truly began. I could hear more Guard members arriving out front. They had been alerted of my presence. The guard advanced. My hybrid selves were elated. It had been so long since **they** had been able to hunt and **they** could not wait.

They lunged forward. The Guard at the front was caught unprepared. He went down easily. I warned **them** not to get too carried away. I wanted to get out alive, and with as little casualties as possible. The first few Guard members fell without putting up much of a fight. Once the others realized what was going on, that I had *changed* and allowed my hybrid forward, they began to *change,* as well. The vampires and werewolves were easy to deal with. The witches were a bit of a problem for me. Luckily for me, Damian woke up. He saw what was going on. He looked at me, surprised. I had told him that I would never let **them** out and here **they** were. I couldn't tell if he was more surprised that **they** were out or by the fact that **they** seemed to be showing control.

Damian had revealed to me that he had a few witch powers of his own. Not very many, but, in this instance, they helped. He was able to create a diversion for the witches, while I took them out. The Guard members on the outside had not realized what was going on inside, yet, but I knew we did not have very much time. I was searching the windows, looking for an exit, when Damian grabbed my hand, being careful of my claws, and led me down the stairs into the basement. My hybrid was still in control, but **they** were being as gentle as possible with Damian. **They,** like me, wanted nothing to happen to him.

He led me to the furthest wall, where a bookshelf was. I couldn't understand why we came to the one place that would be hardest to escape. I made my way toward the small window on the right wall. I could hear other Guard members entering upstairs. I turned around, preparing for another fight, when I felt Damian tugging on my arm.

"Hurry, this way!" Damian said.

I turned around and was surprised to see what appeared to be a tunnel in the floor. I graciously followed him, closing the hatch door above my head as I entered. It was a close call, I could hear the Guard enter the basement as we made our way along the tunnel. My hybrid was not needed at the moment, so I made my way back to the control center of my mind. To my surprise, **they** allowed me to take control without a fight. For once, we had an enemy besides each other.

We travelled along the tunnel for what seemed like hours. Finally making it to the end, we came out where I never would have expected. Damian opened the hatch on the other end, and I stepped out behind him.

"Damian? What are you doing here? The tunnel is only for emergencies!" Someone behind me exclaimed loudly. It was a voice I recognized, but hadn't heard in years. I tried to place a face with the voice. My hybrid was ready to come forward at a moment's notice.

"Sorry, Grandma, but it was… The Guard found us!" Damian said.

"That was faster than I had hoped. Are you both okay?" She asked.

"Yes, we are. Grandmother, this is Avalonia." Damian said, as we turned to look at each other. Up until then I had been looking out the window, trying to see where we were.

"It is a pleasure to meet you." I said turning and reaching out my hand. I stopped short when I saw her face. My wolf growled. My vampire hissed. Even without **them** coming forward, I could feel my eyes start to change.

"You did not tell her who I was." Cassandra, the Witch Council member stated, while looking at her grandson, my Damian.

He was looking at me, shocked at how I was behaving. It took him a few moments before he realized. He remembered the stories I told of my dealings with the Council. He came to my side and grabbed my hand.

"You are safe. She will help us." He said, while using his free hand to rub my back. Something he always did to calm me down.

Slowly, I calmed down. I put my hand back out. "It is nice to see you again, Cassandra." I decided to be a better person. A few years prior I would have tore her apart, without a thought. I had become a better me, though. If she was going to help us, then I would let her. No matter what she did to me in the past, she was Damian's only family, and he was the most important person in my life. If he trusted her, so would I.

"It is nice to see you, too, Avalonia. Though I wish it was under different circumstances." Cassandra said.

Chapter 20

Damian and I spent most of that day with Cassandra, making plans on how to get out of Astoria safely. It was a trying task. I still did not fully trust her. After all, for all I know, she voted to have me killed as a child. I could only hope that Damian was right, that she would help us and not betray us.

Cassandra's plan was very dangerous. She had been planning a trip back to her home in the Witchlands. Her plan was for us to sneak into her vehicle after the Guard had searched it. They had been searching every vehicle that left Astoria, and all that arrived. We would have to leave the safety of her room, and her.

We had set the plan in motion. Damian and I had just made it to the place where we were to meet Cassandra, when we heard the bells. They were holding an emergency Council meeting.

Damian and I looked at each other. We knew now that she wouldn't be coming. There was no way for us to get out of Astoria safely without her.

Damian and I hung out in the alley, behind a trash can, for awhile. Guard members had been patrolling every street. We needed to make a plan.

"We need to get back to her room. It is safe in there." Damian said. I could tell he was trying to sound more sure than he was. He was trying to be brave for me, something that I admired about him.

I wasn't so sure that it was the best idea. With the Council having a meeting, the place would be crawling with the Guard, but Damian said he knew a back way in, a way that would take us safely past the Guard. So, I agreed. That was one of the worst decisions of my life.

We made it back to the Council building with no problems. It took Damian a few minutes to find the door he was looking for, the one that would take us through the walls and back to his grandmother's room. It was hidden well. It matched the brick facade of the building perfectly.

We made our way, as quietly as possible, through the tunnel. I could hear yells, and the stomping of feet, on the outside of the wall. I kept thinking that at any moment we would be found. At any moment they would capture us.

We made it to Cassandra's room with no problems, but, as soon as Damian opened the door, he was grabbed by the Guard. He tried to fight back, but there were too many. He was overpowered within seconds. I didn't have time to react.

My hybrid surged forward. This time **they** didn't wait for permission and I didn't care. We needed to protect our mate. To protect Damian.

I leapt out of the tunnel and attacked the closest guard. He went down quickly, but two more took his place. Every time I took one down, more appeared. It seemed like the entire Guard was there. I was getting tired. My body was taking hit after hit, with no chance to heal. Damian was in the corner. He wasn't moving. I could only tell he was alive by the sound of his breath. I lost concentration for a moment, and that was all the Guard needed. One unexpected blow to the head and I was down. As my eyes closed, I looked at Damian, once more, and prayed that even if I didn't make it, he would.

Chapter 21

Cassandra would later tell me about how the Council had found out that we were there, and about our plan.

Carter and Michael had bugged the rooms of the other Council members. They did not trust them, and they certainly didn't trust each other. They were trying to find a way to get the current members off of the Council, find a way for the people to vote them out. The Council members were the oldest members of each species. The Council members were chosen by age, but the public had a chance, once a year, to vote them out if they thought the Council member was not doing their job correctly.

It was only by sheer luck that they found out about Damian and me. They had just repla the bug in Cassandra's room that day. Wher heard what was going on in there, they cou believe it, they had gotten exactly what they wanted. They had found a reason for the people to take Cassandra off of the Council. An opportunity for them to replace her with someone who is under their control. They also got me.

They waited until Damian and I snuck out of the building, then they made their move. Cassandra was gathering up her things when they entered. It wasn't unusual for the Council members to visit each other, but it was unusual for them to bring members of the Guard with them.

Cassandra looked up, startled. "What is the meaning of this?" She asked, addressing both Michael and Carter. She looked behind them, at the Guard.

"Well, our dear, Cassandra, We heard every detail of your plan to help Avalonia...and was it, Damian?" Carter said, while turning his head to look at Michael, who nodded.

"We are here to arrest you for treason against the state." Michael finished.

Cassandra tried to use her magic to escape when the Guard advanced on her, but her magic would not work.

"Did you think we would just let you use your magic and leave?" Carter asked, laughing. "We thought of that."

They had brought in another witch. His name was Alexander. He was the perfect candidate for them, he loved power and was easy to control.

"Hello, Cassandra." Alexander smiled wickedly at her as he spoke. "It is a pleasure to see you, again."

Cassandra, who was, by this point, in the custody of the Guard, replied. "I wish I could say the same."

Carter laughed at the look on her face, it showed pure hatred of the three of them. "Take her to the Council room, and ring the bells. We need to draw Avalonia and Damian back to us. After all, it is safe here." He said, laughing, as he turned to leave.

The Council meetings were open to the public. As soon as the bell rang, the room began to fill. Everyone there was excited to see why the Council needed an emergency meeting. It was very unusual for them to call one.

It took only a few moments for the remaining Council members, and the Guard, who had Cassandra, to show up. When the crowd saw that Cassandra was in the custody of the Guard, murmurs started. It was getting very loud in the room. The witches were outraged. How dare they capture their representative!

"Quiet!" Michael tried to yell over the crowd. This only seemed to make them louder.

"SILENCE!" Carter boomed. His voice was louder due to the fact that, before he was elected, he was an Alpha.

The crowd quieted instantly. He was the oldest, and, even though the members on the Council were supposed to be equal, he was the one everyone saw as the leader. The most respected.

"We have called this meeting because one of our own," he said, gesturing to Cassandra, "has betrayed us. As most of you know, the past few years, we have been searching for the hybrid, by the name of Avalonia. Cassandra has, just this very day, helped that very hybrid escape."

The crowd roared in outrage. Just as Carter was telling them to quiet down, a Guard member entered and whispered in his ear.

"We have captured them." The Guard member said.

Carter smiled widely. "Excellent, bring them in." He then turned back to the crowd.

Chapter 22

As I slowly woke up, I could hear what sounded to be a large crowd. I was confused. I could not figure out where I was or, for that matter, what was going on. Then I saw Damian. He was looking at me with, what appeared to be, panic in his eyes. I saw two men holding him. That was when I remembered everything that had happened. Once I did remember, my hybrid started to resurface. One of the Guard members noticed my eyes changing color and hit me over the head. The sudden onslaught of pain stopped the *change*.

I took a moment, and just when I was about to try and *change* again, the doors before us opened. I looked up and saw hundreds of people. They all looked toward us. Then I heard his voice. Carter.

"Even though she may have betrayed our trust, our dear Cassandra, could not keep us from catching the hybrid, Avalonia, and her companion. As you can see," he said, gesturing toward the door, "we have them both in custody."

The crowd cheered as we were led to the front of the room. The Guard stopped us right before the Council. That is when Damian and I saw Cassandra. We both started resisting, trying to get away from the Guard. We needed to help her.

Nothing we tried worked. I was unable to *shift*. No matter how much I tried, **they** just could not come forward. More Guard members arrived and helped hold us down.

Once the Guard had me in a position where I couldn't move, I looked at the other members of the Council. The one who had taken Cassandra's seat on the Council was smirking. I could only assume, since he had taken her seat, that he was a witch. Which meant, more than likely, he had something to do with my *shifting* problem.

My vampire and wolf were going crazy. It was one thing for me to lock **them** inside, but for someone else to do it, it was unbearable.

I glared at the Council members. "What is the meaning of this? I have done no crimes! There is no reason to capture us!"

Carter began laughing. The rest of the Council soon followed. The crowd remained silent, waiting to see what was going to happen.

"No crimes? You would have us believe that this is not you? That you never told this story? Never did any of these things?" He questioned, as he gestured to someone behind Damian and me.

All at once, I could hear myself on a recording. I was telling my story. I was saying how my hybrid could not be controlled. How I longed to rip people limb from limb. How I needed them to feel fear. How I wanted them to all be in pain, pain caused by me.

As the recording went on, the people in the crowd started murmuring. Tears were streaming down my face. Not from the Council finding out, but for the simple fact that I had only told that story twice.

I looked over at Damian. He had his head bowed.

"Damian?" I whispered.

He looked up at me, tears streaming down his face. I could see the pain shining through his eyes. My heart rate spiked. The pain was almost too much for me to bear.

"I am so sorry! I wanted my grandmother's help! I took this to her, through the tunnel, the day we went to my house! Before I fell in love with you! I wanted her to understand you! I am so sorry..." He said. The pain in his voice still haunts me.

I closed my eyes and turned my head. I was upset and hurt. How could he betray me? My very mate? The one who was supposed to love me and be with me eternally? I couldn't look at him. Not right then.

"Please, Ava, don't hate me." Damian whispered.

I looked back at him. His eyes were begging me to understand. Begging me to forgive him. "I could never hate you. I love you Damian"

In the background I could hear myself say...

"And now I have **them** locked up. I am, finally, in control."

Everyone was so entranced in my story that they didn't hear Damian and me talking. I had no idea what was to become of me, but I knew, no matter what, I would save Damian.

"There you have it, everyone. Avalonia, the monster hybrid herself, just told us all, in her own words, how dangerous she is. That is why we have been trying to find her, all these years. I know I, for one, feel safer knowing that she is now in the custody of the Guard." Carter said, as the crowd cheered.

"She has it under control! Her hybrid sides are no longer a factor! She is not a danger to anyone!" Damian shouted out. It earned him a hard kick to the side of the head.

I growled. The emotional trauma of them hitting my mate was the one thing the witch's magic couldn't conquer. My hybrid selves came forward. I let **them**. I threw a Guard member off of me and took out the ones holding Damian. I knew I couldn't fight the magic much longer. More and more witches were joining in to stop me.

"Run! Damian!" I screamed through the pain of another hit from the Guard.

"I will not leave you!" Damian shouted back. His eyes held determination.

"Damian, please! Go to my pack! Tell my father! I can't hold them much longer." I said. Begging him to see in my eyes the need for him to be safe.

I looked back at him, briefly. I could see conflict in his eyes. He didn't want to leave me. Then, finally, resolution. He turned and fled back toward the door. Some people tried to stop him, but he was able to use what little magic he had to keep them off. I watched him vanish out the door. I was growing weak, and tired. My body was giving out. I knew that I needed to hold them off for as long as possible. Damian needed a fair chance to get away.

I held them off for a few minutes, which seemed like an eternity. Finally, my body and mind couldn't take the combined onslaught from the witches and Guard any longer, it gave out, and, once more, everything went black.

Chapter 23

Damian told me later, that it only took him a day to reach my Packlands. As soon as he had escaped the building, he found his grandmother's car. He knew that Cassandra always kept a spare key, hidden by magic, in the rear wheel well.

He drove all night and when he made it to the border, he didn't stop. He blew right past the patrol wolves and headed straight toward the pack house.

My father was already outside. One of the border wolves ran ahead to tell him that someone was coming into their lands.

Damian slammed on the brakes when he saw them standing there. He left the ignition on, as he jumped out.

My father was pissed that someone had come onto his land without permission, but once he saw that it was Damian, and that he was alone, his anger turned to fear.

"Avalonia is in trouble." Damian spit out, not taking the time to speak properly to an Alpha. Some of the the pack growled at the disrespect.

My father's fears grew. "What has happened? Where is she?" He asked.

Damian replied. "The Council has her. I made a huge mistake the day after we left here. I recorded our conversation about her hybrid and took it to my grandmother. Somehow, the rest of the Council found out about it. They have been searching for us. They had us captured, but Avalonia used the rest of her strength so I could escape. They still have her. You have to help!"

By this time, most of the pack had gathered around. My mother had also joined my father. Damian took his eyes off of my father to look at her when she started hissing. Her vampire was in full control. She tried to lunge at Damian. If he had not made the recording, none of this would be happening. To my mother, my capture was all Damian's fault.

My father grabbed her and held her. "Melovanin, since he is here, since he came all this way, we have to trust that he is only here to help us get our daughter back." He said. My father told me later that he didn't fully trust Damian, but he had no choice but to believe him in that instant. If I was truly in danger and he did not act, he would never forgive himself.

He then turned to the pack. "Our daughter, Avalonia, is in trouble. I will not stand by while the Council holds my daughter captive. She has done nothing wrong. I will not order you to join me, but I would accept anyone who is willing to."

My mother said. "I will call the coven. They will come to her aid. She is the future Súmaire." She turned and ran into the house.

Damian was silent through it all. Looking at them admiringly. They were great leaders in his eyes and, it appeared, even better parents. They would risk the wrath of the Council, and even their world, to save their daughter.

"My grandmother has some loyal witch friends. I may be able to get them to help, as well, if I could use your phone." Damian said to my father.

"Of course. Anything to help Avalonia." My father said. He only hoped Damian was telling the truth and that these witches he was calling were going to help them, and not some form of an elaborate trap. He turned back to the pack, who had been discussing amongst themselves whether they would help or not. "We do not have much time. WIll you help your future Luna? Or not?" My father asked.

The pack looked from my father to Damian. My father had figured out, the last time we were there, that Damian was my mate. What wolf or vampire would risk so much for a human? He knew even before I did. Therefore, human or not, he would be the next Alpha of the pack.

The pack smiled. They let out a war cry as a sign of consent. They would help save their Luna.

It took my mother, father, and Damian almost twelve hours to gather up as many people as possible. The Guard was vast, and, if they wanted to save me and go against them, they would need an army.

It took them another day to reach Astoria. The witches and vampires met them there. Our coven had recruited another coven to help. My parents and Damian had their army.

They attacked the Capital Building at noon. The Guard was changing shifts. They had organized the pack, witches, and vampires into sections. The plan was to use a wave approach. The vampires, who were the fastest, would attack first. Then the witches, with their magic. Finally, the werewolves, they were the strongest.

The vampires stormed into the building. The Guard was caught unaware. By the time they had figured out what was happening, most of the vampires had slipped past. Some were coming to try and get me out, the others were headed for the Council. If they were attacking the Council, they had to do it right. A full blown takeover.

My parents and Damian were the last ones to enter the building. They had the hardest job. They had to make it to Carter's office. It was the hardest to reach, therefore, all the Council members would have retreated there.

Luckily, my parents had been there before. They both stayed in front of Damian and protected him, as they fought their way through the masses. Once they made it to the staircase that went up to Carter's office, my father went first, then Damian, and, lastly, my mother. They wanted to be covered on all sides.

The door to Carter's office was barred. My father had to *shift* into his wolf and use all of his strength to bust it down. The Council was prepared. As soon as he entered, he was hit by a spell. He was down and couldn't move. Damian was a little more cautious. He tried to fire a spell back into the room, but his magic was no match for Alexander, the new witch Council member. It took three spells, but Damian went down as well.

My mother's vampire was in full control. Most of the time, vampires only care about one thing: their own safety. Their own survival. There is one exception to that rule: when a vampire finds their mate and has a child, the safety of their mate and child becomes the most important thing. When my father went down, my mother lost all control. She went into autopilot mode, in a sense. Without a rational thought, she charged into the room. She made it far enough into the room to take a swipe at Alexander, but she was not quick enough to miss his spell. Within a moment, she was down as well.

The Council took advantage and tied them all up. Alexander kept casting a spell that made them immobile. They were now at the mercy of the Council.

Chapter 24

After the Guard took me out, the first thing I remember, upon waking up, was not knowing where I was. I was disoriented. My vision was blurry.

"We are in the cells in the basement." I heard a voice say. It took me a moment to find the person it was attached to. Cassandra was in a cell beside mine. The cell had been charmed, so that she could not use magic to escape.

"Cassandra? Are you okay?" I asked her. "How long have we been here?"

"I am fine. Just over a day. I was beginning to think you would never wake up." She said. "Thank you for saving Damian, by the way."

"You never have to thank me for anything that concerns Damian." I said back, while trying to look for any way to escape.

I looked back at her. She was smiling widely. She opened her mouth to speak, when a Guard member entered the room and she quickly closed it. She glared at him. I could tell she, like me, wanted to make each and every Guard member pay. She was full of hatred.

"I better not hear another word out of you two. I could hear you all the way at the top of the stairs. Prisoners are not allowed to speak to each other." He said. "If I hear it again, you both will get to meet my dear friend Betsy."

He held up a stick that was shooting sparks. Cassandra gasped. I had no idea what it was, but could only assume it was filled with magic. He laughed and went to sit at the Guard desk. He propped his feet up and stared at us both. He beamed. Daring either of us to say a word.

I went to open my mouth to speak. Cassandra began to frantically shake her head. I closed my mouth and just looked at her. If she was scared to speak, I could assume that I should be, too. Since she was a Council member, she had intimate knowledge of all the weapons the Guard had.

The cells were quiet. The Guard had fallen asleep, but Cassandra and I still did not speak. After a while, Cassandra fell asleep.

It was the next morning when I heard signs of fighting. I knew that Damian had come through for us.

"Cassandra." I whispered. Trying to wake her up. "Cassandra!"

She finally stirred. "What is it, now?" She asked, still half asleep.

"Damian has brought my pack and coven. I can hear them upstairs. Be prepared. We may have to fight." I told her. My hybrid sides were excited. **They** wanted to fight.

I could hear footsteps on the stairs, whether friend or foe, I didn't know. I did not recognize their scent. I was ready, either way. They were getting closer. I began to growl. They hissed. A moment later, Mavis, one of my coven members turned the corner.

"Growling is not the way to greet your rescue party. Especially, when they are a vampire." He said, while trying to get into my cell, which was easier said than done. The cells were made for supernaturals. He finally found a key in the Guard desk, the guard having deserted it when the commotion upstairs started, and let me out.

"I am sorry, Mavis. I was preparing for a fight, in case you were an enemy." I said, taking the key from him and opening Cassandra's cell.

"Thank you." Cassandra said.

I turned back toward Mavis. "Where are my parents and Damian?" I asked. I needed to find them. I needed to make sure Damian was safe. My hybrid and I were going insane not knowing if he was okay.

"Don't even think about it. My orders were to take you out of here. You are not to join in the fight." He said, grabbing my arm, trying to pull me in the opposite direction of the stairs.

My hybrid took this as an insult. We would fight whether they wanted **us** to or not. I could feel **them** pushing forward even more.

"TELL **US** NOW!" **They** said, grabbing the front of his shirt.

Mavis began to cower. He may have been older, but I was his future Súmaire, he had no choice but to obey me, even if it meant going against my mother. I could tell he was trying to fight it.

152

"Fine. I will tell you, but I am going with you." He said.

"So am I." Cassandra said. Magic was sparking from her fingers. She was ready.

Mavis looked from her to me. "They all went to Carter's office. He will be the hardest to take out, your parents wanted the pleasure of doing it." He said.

I shook my head, I should have known they would go after the head of the Council. I looked to Cassandra. "Do you know where his office is?" I asked her. I knew that Carter would be well protected. We needed to get there to help my parents and Damian, as soon as possible.

"Yes, follow me." She said, as she started up the stairs. Mavis and I followed.

We went up three flights of stairs, and entered into chaos. Bodies were being thrown everywhere. Werewolf, vampire, witch, and Guard members were battling it out in the conference room. We needed to get to the other side of the room to get up to Carter's office. We had to fight our way through.

We dove into battle. Cassandra was throwing spells at any Guard member she saw. They had made a severe mistake by arresting the oldest most powerful witch. Mavis was doing just as well. Guard member after Guard member went down.

I jumped on the first Guard member I saw. He had another vampire, that I didn't know, on the ground, going for the killing blow. I was able to take him down and save the vampire. She was grateful. She looked young, like she had just *turned*. Once I knew she was safe, I attacked the next Guard member, then another, and another. Before I knew it, I was on the other side of the room. Cassandra and Mavis were not far behind.

I ran up the stairs toward Carter's office. The sounds of the battle below were fading, only to be replaced by the sounds of laughter from above. If my parents and Damian were in Carter's office, something had to have been wrong. I picked up my pace. Mavis had caught up to me. Cassandra was still close to the bottom of the stairs.

Mavis and I entered the room to see my parents and Damian against the far wall. Damian was bleeding profusely from the head. My father saw me and his eyes bugged.

Carter, and the other Council members, had not noticed that we had entered. They still had their backs to us.

I heard Carter say, "You just thought that you could walk in here and take over. That we wouldn't be prepared. I have the best witches anyone could want! The Guard is made up of the best fighters in the lands! You could not possibly think that your plan would work!" He said, while laughing, the other Council members joined him. The witch, Alexander, looked smug. Carter had called him the best. His ego was too large.

By this point, Cassandra had joined us. She did not like Carter's "best witches" comment, at all, judging by the look on her face. Before Mavis or I could stop her she stepped forward.

"I will show you the best witch, Carter." With that said, she let out a spell toward them all. At the last second, Alexander, countered it.

"You have to be better than that, Cassandra." He laughed, while shooting a spell back at her. She countered his. It turned into an all-out battle of spells.

Carter had, finally, realized that I was there. His face went from laughing to angry, in a second flat.

"How did you get out? You were put in a cell in the basement. Where is the Guard member assigned to you?" He said.

"Not even going to mention Cassandra getting out?" I asked. I was inching my way closer to Damian. I needed to make sure he was alright. The wound on his head hadn't stopped bleeding. Mavis was right beside me. "Or how we got past all the Guard members downstairs? Your security is slipping." I taunted. Each word took me closer to Damian.

"I do not care about Cassandra. You are who they want." Carter said, as he kicked toward my parents and Damian. Who were still behind him. He hit Damian in the knee. Even in his comatose state, he let out an exhalation of pain.

I made the mistake of hissing and growling. Doing both at the same time was a feat, even for me. Carter caught on, right away. He had thought that Damian and I may be emotionally close, since we were captured together, but it was my growl-hiss reaction, when he kicked Damian, that helped him put it together. Since he was a werewolf himself, he knew of mates. He had figured out that Damian was mine. As soon as I realized Carter's intention, I lunged forward, but I was too far away. Carter grabbed Damian before I could reach him. My growls grew louder. Mavis began hissing. He had also figured out that Damian was my mate. Damian was his future leader, his Súmaise.

Carter grabbed Damian by the neck. I backed off. I was helpless. Damian couldn't fight back. He was still unconscious. I couldn't do anything, or Carter would only hurt him more.

"Well, well, well. The hybrid has a heart." He taunted. "Who would ever have thought that such a killer could ever love? I will make you a deal: you join me and the Council, as a special enforcer, and I let your precious mate live. What do you say?" He asked, while squeezing Damian's neck even harder. Damian's face was changing colors.

I let out another growl. My father and mother had slowly been making their way behind Carter. They had used my distraction as a way to get free. Carter had not noticed that they had moved while he was talking to me. My father stood up and nodded his head at me. He was letting me know that he would do anything he could to save Damian, while I took out Carter. It was my fight. I couldn't help but smile a little at my father. He had my back, and knew that Carter was mine to take out, even if he wanted the honor.

Just as I was about to speak, Cassandra rejoined us. She had won her battle. Alexander lay on a heap in the floor. Michael, whom I had long since forgotten about, sat beside him, apparently checking on him. The Vampire Council member was leaning against the wall. He, like most vampires, was just worried about himself, he was waiting to see who would come out on top.

Carter took my smile as acceptance. He began to smile, too, and, thankfully, eased off of Damian's neck.

"I am so glad you have decided to join us. Now, you must do your first assignment." He smirked. Then looked at Mavis and Cassandra. "Kill them." He said.

I pretended like I agreed. I nodded my head. Carter thought I was nodding at him, I was truly nodding at my father. As soon as I nodded, my father and I both sprang into action. I started forward. Carter, caught off guard, lost his grip on Damian. My father took the opportunity and grabbed Damian, putting him behind himself and my mother. My mother began to check on him.

I reached Carter, as soon as Damian was safe. I knocked him to the ground. Carter quickly made the *change* from human to wolf. My wolf wanted to take full control. **She** wanted to test her strength against Carter. My vampire also wanted to take full control. **They** both held a grudge against him, for locking **them** up and wanting to kill **us**. I thought, at first, **they** were going to fight each other in my mind, but then Carter charged. **They** made the decision quickly to share the glory, to share the battle. **They** quickly attacked Carter. **They** were vicious. He had wronged **us**, and had threatened and hurt **our** mate, he had to be taken out. The battle raged on. It was on par with the internal battle between my hybrid and me. Carter lunged again and took a chunk out of my leg. My wolf howled. My vampire hissed. **They** didn't let it affect **them** very much. Within a second, **they** dived forward and bit his leg. He howled and tried to pull away. **Their** grip just got tighter. **They** were channeling all the anger **they** felt into that bite.

Carter finally shook **them** loose. He was limping, badly, as **they** circled him. I had to watch the battle from inside my mind since I let **them** take full control. It was surreal.

Carter had become more cautious. He would spring forward, then retreat, hoping to get a lucky shot. My hybrid sides were enjoying **themselves**. Finally, **they** tired of the game and rushed forward. Since **they** had not done anything offensive in a while, Carter was caught off guard. It made it easy for **them** to bite the largest and closest target: his neck.

Carter gave up almost as soon as **they** grabbed his neck. **They** wanted to kill him, to tear him to shreds. I couldn't allow that. **We** needed to prove that **we** had grown, that **we** were not a monster. That **we** were not who Carter made **us** out to be. **We** were not a killer.

I began to push my way forward. At first, **they** resisted. **They** had blood and flesh in **their** mouth. **They** wanted to make him pay.

"Please, **we** are not killers. Think of Damian. Would he want this? Would he approve? **Our** mate needs **us**. Please!" I pleaded with **them** in my mind. It took a moment, but **they** finally stopped resisting and slipped back into my mind. **They** knew, as much as I, that Damian wouldn't want **us** to kill.

I released Carter's neck. My father looked at me, surprised. Apparently, he had assumed, since I let **them** back out, that **they** would try to stay in control. I was surprised that **they** had complied, as well.

In that moment, I felt as if I was truly free. **We** were finally one.

Chapter 25

I made sure that Carter was fully subdued before I ran to Damian. I wanted, and needed, to check on him right away, but, if Carter was still a threat, I could not leave him. My father took control of Carter. By this point, other vampires, witches, and werewolves had joined us in the room. The battle downstairs with the Guard had also been won.

Damian was still unconscious when I reached him. I gently placed his head on my lap. I needed him to be all right. I needed him to wake up. I needed him. I began to cry.

Cassandra soon joined me. She, like me, needed to make sure her adversary was taken out. Three other witches had Alexander in custody. She looked at her grandson's body and began saying a spell, over and over again. She was getting more desperate by the minute. After about fifteen long, horrible minutes, she stopped. She slouched over Damian's body and began to cry.

By this time, my tears had stopped. Anger began to take the place of sadness. Someone would have to pay for this. I laid Damian's head down and started to get up. My father still had a hold on Carter, he saw what was happening. My hybrid sides were furious and wanted Carter's head. For once, I fully agreed with them.

My father pushed Carter behind him. I growled loudly. At this point, I would do anything to get to my prey. I tried to go around my father. We were circling each other. He made sure to keep Carter behind himself at all times. Everyone else in the room was silent. All that could be heard were my growls and snarls, and Cassandra's weeping.

"Avalonia, think about what you are doing. This is not you. Damian is alive. What would he want you to do?" My father asked me. He was trying to use the same logic on me, as I had on my hybrid selves.

"Bringing Damian into this isn't going to get me to stop. He may never wake up. Carter did that. He deserves everything he will get and more. He may not have killed Damian, but he has destroyed more people's lives than anyone else on the Council. He is the mastermind behind everything that goes on here! He deserves to DIE!" By the end

I was screaming. On the word die, I charged. I needed to destroy Carter. He needed to pay for what he had done to Damian.

My father did not move. He stayed in front of Carter. When I lunged, I hit him instead. My mother hissed. My father didn't even try to fight back. I was scratching and biting, taking all my frustrations out on him, since I could not get past him, to Carter. My father just let me. He was an Alpha, so he healed extremely quickly. Every blow I landed healed within seconds.

I was emotionally drained and was quickly becoming physically drained, as well. A few more blows and my body tired. I couldn't keep up this assault on my father. One final hit and I collapsed. My father caught me. He held me tight. He held me like his, and my, life depended on it. He held me like he did when I was scared as a child. He held me as I cried.

"Thank you." I said, once I had finally calmed down and was thinking rationally again, which was hard to do, since I did not have my mate there to calm me.

My father held me tighter, and said, "You don't ever have to thank me. I knew you would regret it if I let you kill again. Right now, your mate needs you. Let me handle this."

I pulled away and looked at my father, I saw worry in his eyes. He was worried about me. After what had just happened, and what I had went through in the past, I could not blame him. I was unstable. I looked toward Damian and nodded my head. I needed to get him somewhere safe. Somewhere that he would, hopefully, recover.

I let go of my father and walked toward Damian and Cassandra. A few other witches had gathered around to try and help. They all were chanting different spells. None of them worked.

My mother looked at me. I knew what she was going to suggest. We could both hear Damian's heart rate slowing. I had to make one of the hardest decisions that I have ever made. Would I let my mate die? Or would I attempt to turn him into a vampire?

I needed Cassandra's help. Damian would not be happy with me if I didn't ask her first. She was his only family. I was his mate, but until we were married I was not considered family by any of the species.

"Cassandra, I need to talk with you." I said. "Cassandra." I repeated just a little bit louder, when she didn't move. Finally, she looked up and nodded her head.

I helped her stand up. We walked to the farthest corner of the room. I could hear my father, and the witches, in the background. I could also hear Damian's heart rate slow even further. We did not have much time.

"Have you ever heard of a partial witch being turned into a vampire?" I asked her.

She had been staring at Damian, with my words, her head snapped straight to me.

"No." She whispered. "No! I won't allow it." She was shaking her head violently.

"Cassandra, I can hear his heartbeat slowing. None of the spells are working. I need to do this. I can't lose him. I don't know if witches have *mates*, but he is mine." When I said this, she looked deep into my eyes. I hoped she could see the truth, see how much I loved Damian, see how lost I would be without him. "I refuse to let him die without trying everything I possibly can. My father will be the new wolf Council member, so he will say yes. The vampire Marcus will allow it, because we allowed him to live. Whoever the new human is will have no say in it. All I need is your permission. I am trying to do this the right way. Please, Cassandra, do not make me go against you, because with, or without, your permission, I will try to save my mate. Our Damian." I said, begging her to allow it.

She looked into my eyes. Tears were running down both of our faces. She looked back at Damian. Than she nodded her head yes.

"Thank you!" I said, while hugging her. I moved as fast as I could toward Damian. My mother met me there. She helped me carry him out of the office. We headed to Cassandra's office. I wanted to take Damian to his house, through the tunnel. Being surrounded by his things would, hopefully, help make the transition easier.

I had never seen a human, or partial witch, transformed into a vampire before. It was a very rare occurrence, nowadays, for anyone to be turned. Most vampires were born.

It took us only a few minutes to make it to Damian's house. We had used our vampire speed to get there. We took Damian up to the master bedroom. The very same bedroom we had been so happy in, a few days before.

We laid Damian on the bed. My mother then went around and closed the blinds. New vampires were extremely sensitive to light and all vampires who were not inducted into my mother's coven were unable to walk in the sunlight. Once they had went through a ceremony and were placed as a member in her coven, they like her and the other coven members were able to walk in the sun.

My mother had done this before, so, I let her take the lead. She moved over to Damian and hovered over him.

"Hold open his mouth." She instructed me.

I grabbed his jaw and forced it open as gently as I could. His jaw was locked into place. I almost broke it. I bit my lip to keep myself from crying out in the pain, I could only assume, he was in.

My mother then bit into her own wrist. She moved it over his mouth. Blood began to pour into Damian's throat. With her other hand, my mother massaged Damian's throat. We needed the blood to go down. It would do no good if he was unable to swallow it and get it into his system.

She kept reopening her wrist and giving him blood for around ten minutes. I was afraid he wasn't going to last through it. His heart rate grew weaker and weaker by the minute. I couldn't stop the tears from running down my face.

At the eleven minute mark his heart stopped completely. It was then that I broke down. I couldn't stand. I collapsed over him. I wrapped my arms around him and snuggled, as closely as I could.

I knew the process would take hours, maybe even days. We would have to wait and see if it even worked. I would not, and could not, give up hope.

My mother left soon after his heart stopped, she knew I needed to be alone with him. My father would need her help getting the Council back together, also. Once the masses found out that the Council had been taken over, there would be a panic. They needed to fix everything before that happened. I was in no state to help. For now, I was useless. I would stay with my mate.

Chapter 26

After I left with my mother, my father and Cassandra started to take control and reset the Council. Carter's office, my father's new office, since he was next in line after Carter, was abuzz. Vampires, witches, and werewolves had gathered in.

"Attention." My father began. When the crowd didn't quiet down, he repeated, louder, "Atthhhhentionhhh!" It came out as a growl. Everyone quieted, immediately.

"Since Carter and Michael are no longer able to fill their positions, I will be taking mine. We need to find out who of the humans is next in line. We need to do this quickly. We can not have the masses panicking. We all remember what it was like before the Council." The people in the room all nodded their heads.

***

Before the Council was formed, the World was in chaos. Wars were breaking out everywhere. Small factions broke off in each species. Some of the supernatural species thought they were better than the others. Then the Great Supernatural War came. The war that united the supernatural creatures against the humans. The war lasted for years. Many died on both sides. A few of the supernaturals, from each species, secretly met and came up with the plan for the Council. They sent the oldest of the three species on a goodwill mission to meet with the humans. It took months, but the humans finally agreed to the plan. Then, all that was left was to convince the rest of the supernaturals.

The representatives of each species sent out people to recruit more supporters. They kept recruiting until they had an army. The three supernatural armies banded together with the humans. They didn't want to kill their brothers, but, to stop the perpetual wars, they had to. They had one final battle, in what today is known as Astoria, the capital of our world. In the end, the members who would form the Council and their armies won. That is how the Council was formed.

***

Everyone got to work quickly. Michael had been taken to the dungeons. My father, Cassandra, and Marcus, the vampire Council member, went down to talk to him. Michael was the only one who knew who was next in line for the humans. The

Council set it that way for the safety of that person. Others may try to kill him, and take his position. My father did not trust Marcus, but he had not fought in the battle, so, his position on the Council was still set.

They gathered around Michael's cell. My father was the first to speak.

"Michael, we need to know who is next in line. You are the only one who knows. For the Council to be complete, we need a human representative." My father said.

Michael was sitting with his head bowed. He glanced up when my father finished talking.

"There was a time when I would do anything for the people. Then I met Carter. He molded me into the man I am today. He tried to mold the entire Council to fulfill his needs. He cares more about the power and prestige that the title gives him than the people." He said. "I will tell you who he is, on one condition: you put me somewhere far away from Carter."

My father looked at him. He could tell Michael was sincere. He looked at Cassandra and Marcus, they all agreed.

"Very well. Tell us who he is and, as soon as possible, we will move you to another location.

Far away from Carter." As he said the last line, he turned toward Carter's cell. "As for you, Carter, you will rot in this cell. I am sure Marcus will be more than willing to tell us all of your dirty little secrets. I am sure we will find more than one reason to keep you locked up. For good."

Carter just stared at my father. He had nothing left to say.

"Now, Michael, tell us who he is." My father said turning back to Michael.

Michael sighed, "His name is Tobias Smith. He lives about six miles from here."

My father looked at Marcus. "Will you look in the register and find this man? We need him here as soon as we can get him."

Marcus nodded his head, then turned around and left.

Cassandra and my father left orders with a vampire named Marie to move Michael to the other side of the dungeons. The dungeons stretched for miles under Astoria, Michael would be far away from Carter.

After leaving the dungeons, my father and Cassandra headed upstairs. They needed to see who amongst the Guard would be loyal to them. As they entered the Council meeting room, it was crowded with those who had fought on our side, and the Guard members, who had fought for the Council.

My father looked around. The Guard were in the middle of the room, surrounded by the vampires, witches, and werewolves who had fought with us. My father made his way to the Council seats at the head of the room. Once there, he looked out over the crowd. Most had seen him enter and were looking his way. He walked up to the mic and tapped his hand on the top of it. The stage was the only part of the room not damaged in battle.

My father cleared his throat, then said, "As most of you know, we have overthrown the old Council members. We have all known that they were corrupt. They blackmailed a lot of people to stay in their positions. It is also believed that Carter killed his predecessor, Malaki. Without evidence, we could not do anything about that. Over the years, Carter and Michael became more corrupt. They wanted to keep their seats of power. Even when they were supposed to step down, and let the new Council members take their positions. Today, we have done that job for them. I will, finally, be taking my place on the Council. Marcus and Cassandra will remain in theirs. The human seat will be filled, as soon as we locate its owner. My question, now, goes out to the Guard members.

WIll you accept this change, as it was meant to be? Or are you corrupt, like Carter and Michael? Will you join us in protecting our world?" My father asked.

Everyone in the room turned to the Guard. The Guard members looked at each other. All waiting for the others to make a move. Finally, an older Guard member moved to the front.

"I don't know about the others, but I, for one, am sick to death of Carter. His reign has been too long." He said. Then, as is customary when new Council members are appointed, he took off his helmet, laid it on the floor at his feet, went down on one knee and bowed. Pledging himself to the new Council. It wasn't long before the rest of the Guard joined him.

"Very well then. We need to clean this place up. In a few hours, people from all lands will be here. We need to make sure they do not see the chaos that was caused here, this night." My father said. He then turned and headed toward his new office, Cassandra followed. Once there, he assessed the damage. The most important battle had taken place in here and it had taken it's toll on the room. My father and Cassandra began to clean up. It was a few minutes after they began, when Marcus entered.

"I have found him. I have sent a vampire and a Guard member to his house. They should return shortly." Marcus said.

"Thank you." My father said. "Please, have someone send him up here, when he arrives. We should all talk. The future of our world is now in our hands. I, for one, want to make it a better one." Marcus nodded, then left to tell the Guard.

"I have never wanted this position, but, now that I am here, I am glad. I finally have the opportunity to set right all the wrongs Carter has done." My father said to Cassandra.

"I believe you will do an excellent job. Seeing you grow as an Alpha has proved to me that you will not let the power go to your head. You will always do what you believe is right for the people." Cassandra said.

My father bowed his head. He had a slight smile on his face. To hear those words from Cassandra, one of the few people he respected on the Council, meant a lot to him and his confidence as a leader.

About that time, Marcus returned. He was followed by a human man.

"You must be Tobias." My father said. "I am Donavon. Please, have a seat. We all need to talk." He gestured to seats around his desk.

"I wasn't informed as to why I was brought here. Would you tell me? My wife is worried. I would like to be able to abate her fears when I leave here." Tobias said, as he looked around at them all. "I am leaving, right?"

My father was appalled. "Of course you are leaving! You are the new human Council member. That is all we needed you here for. We need to talk about what we are to tell the public. They will be frantic at the sudden change of members."

Tobias let out a sigh of relief. He never expected that to be the reason he would be here. "I didn't realize I was next in line. Even so, what happened to the other Council members? Carter and Michael? Why have they stepped down so suddenly?" He asked.

My father stood up and went to look out the window. He took a deep breath and began. "I am not sure how aware you were of their treacheries. I have explained this all to the Guard, a little while ago. Carter and Michael, have been blackmailing people to stay in their positions. They were supposed to retire years ago. Everyone was too afraid of them to do anything. Until now. They arrested my daughter for nothing. Marcus told me they were planning on putting her to death, this morning. I could not stand by and allow that to happen. A lot of others agreed. We stormed the building, at noon, yesterday, and we won the battle. Now, it is up to us, the new Council members, to set it straight for the public. We need to find a way to make it less hostile for them."

Tobias sat silently as my father spoke. By the end he was in shock. He, like many others, believed that the Council was always doing the right thing for the people. He had no idea anything like that had been going on.

My father gave him a moment to gather his thoughts. Then, my father and the Council sat down and had a meeting. It lasted for nearly five hours. By this time, the sun was high in the sky.

The Guard had been escorting people into the building for well over an hour. The place was packed. Every seat was full. Almost every empty space was filled with people standing. It was abuzz with chatter. Everyone was wondering why the Council had suddenly gotten new members. Normally they had an elaborate ceremony to bring in the new, and take out the old. It was a tradition that dates back to the forming of the Council.

My father and the other Council members entered the room. As soon as they entered, a silence fell over the room. My father looked around at the massive crowd. It was his job to speak to the crowd. A werewolf was the first member of the original Council and, since then, they had been the designated head of the Council.

My father cleared his throat. "I know all of you are wondering why we have had the sudden change of Council members. We had a meeting before we came out here and have decided to tell you all the truth. Carter and Michael were corrupt." Voices raised in outrage. The people needed proof before they would believe. Lucky for my father, the very devices Carter and Michael installed had given them that proof.

Since Carter and Michael didn't trust each other, they had each installed cameras that the other knew nothing about. Therefore, there was footage, that Marcus recovered, of them doing various devious activities.

"Please, everyone, quiet down." My father said. "We have all the proof we needed to arrest them both. If you will direct your attention to the back wall. We will be showing you some of the proof we have. So that you will be able to see, for yourselves, what they have done." He motioned toward the Guard to start the video.

***

The video began with Carter sitting at his desk, doing paperwork. A moment later, a Guard member entered with a man. My father knew this man well. It was my grandfather.

"Carter, here is Mathias." The Guard member said.

"Thank you. You may leave us." Carter waved his hand in dismissal.

"What is the meaning of this, Carter? You have me woken up, in the middle of the night, and dragged here, the day before the ceremony for me to take over for you! Why?" My grandfather demanded to know.

Carter smiled. "I dragged you here to tell you that I am not stepping down. You will forfeit your right to be on the Council. I have it on good authority that, after your mate died, you have had relations with another female. This, you know, is punishable by death. Once we mate, we mate for life. That means yours, as well as hers. So, you will step down, or you will be tried, and I will see to it that you do get the death sentence."

My grandfather was speechless. He had only slipped up once since my grandmother had passed. It was with another widowed wolf. They both had been feeling lonely and wanted the company. They had a few drinks and, before you know it, they awoke in bed together the next morning. Both vowed to never say a word to anyone, but somehow Carter had found out.

"What will it be, Mathias? Death, or your seat on the Council? You decide. Now." Carter said, with a wicked gleam in his eye.

My grandfather slumped in his chair. He knew the battle was lost. He shook his head, sighed, and said, "I will give up my seat. As long as I have your word that no one will find out what you know."

Carter's smile grew. "Of course, no one shall ever find out." Then he turned to the door and said. "Guard, please escort Mathias home."

Once my grandfather left, Michael entered. Carter then relayed what had happened. Michael then told him a similar story, that had coincided his own. They then had a drink. Neither knowing that the other had bugged their room.

Everyone in the room knew what had happened next. My grandfather and the human, who were supposed to be the new Council members, both came to the ceremony and declined the honor of being a Council member. This meant that Carter and Michael would remain in their positions until it was time for my grandfathers and the humans positions to be up.

As soon as they had uttered the words of rejection, my grandfather and the human were arrested. Carter and Michael did not want any witnesses left of their treachery. A few weeks later, after a lengthy trial, my grandfather and the human were put to death.

***

The crowd was silent. Nobody had known of the circumstances of their deaths. The story my grandfather had told was true. Yes, he woke up in bed next to a woman who wasn't his mate, but he had no recollection of actually being intimate with her. With this new information, some began to consider that Carter and Michael had planned it all. A way to ensure their reign. Maybe they were right.

My father cleared his throat to get the crowds attention. "There is the proof you wanted. Do you see, now, why we had to get them out of the Council?" He paused, to give the crowd a moment to think. "We want to build a better Council. We want to build a Council on trust, loyalty, and truth. We will never lie to you. We will always be loyal to our people. We will always do our best to show this in many ways. We will be a just Council. A Council you deserve!"

The crowd remained silent for a moment, seemingly still in shock. Then the room exploded. Voices were raised in outrage and joy. Everyone agreed that they needed a new Council. The people were happy.

That is how my father, Cassandra, Marcus, and Tobias, became, in my opinion, and many others, the greatest Council we have ever had.

Chapter 27

I awoke early the next morning. Damian was still silent beside me. I had cried so much, through the night, that I had dried tears stuck to my face. Damian's shirt was soaked, as well.

I laid next to him for awhile, watching him. I kept hoping for a sign that it was working, even though my mother said that I wouldn't see any until it actually worked. He would either wake up or he wouldn't. I chose to believe that, if he was in there fighting, he would show me a sign. I hoped he would be able to.

I slowly crawled out of bed. It took all of my willpower. My hybrid had retreated to the darkest recesses of my mind. **They** couldn't handle having Damian like this. Before, **they** could sense him. Then, nothing. I knew Damian wouldn't want me to do this to myself. All he ever wanted was for me to be happy, but I knew, for a fact, that if he didn't wake up, I never would be again, at least not fully.

I had just gotten out of the shower, and into clothes, when my parents showed up. I heard them coming, but gave them no indication that I had.

"Avalonia?" My father questioned, walking into the room.

I was sitting on a chair in the corner of the room, staring at Damian. I looked up at my father, as he drew near. He kneeled down in front of me and gave me a hug. He just held me as I cried.

My mother was checking on Damian. It had been almost twenty four hours since my mother had given him blood. We both hoped that the *change* would happen quickly. After she was done checking on him, she came over to me. My father moved out of the way, so that she could hug me. By this point, my eyes were dry. No matter how much I wanted to cry, nothing would come out. My mother noticed this.

"Avalonia, I know you will not leave, but will you, please, eat something? You must keep your strength up. You can not do this to yourself. Damian needs you to be strong." My mother begged.

I couldn't talk, so I just nodded my head yes. She turned to my father and told him what to get. I saw him leave, out of the corner of my eye. My eyes were still focused on Damian.

My mother sat beside me, and just held my hand. Her silence allowed me to think. My hybrid had hidden, but the rage **they** had for Carter remained. The longer Damian stayed in this state, the more it grew. Even my human side wanted nothing more than to tear apart Carter, if Damian was gone, no one would stop me, could stop me. Carter's blood would be mine.

***

It had been six days since my mother had given Damian her blood. In twenty four hours, it would be day seven. If he did not wake up then, he never would. My hybrid had resurfaced days before. **Their** anger had grown, as had my human side's. As the time of Damian's chances of recovery drew closer to an end, *we* became more violent. No one could enter the room. My parents had been trying to get me to calm down, but, at this point, I was too far gone. I attacked anyone who entered. I hadn't eaten in days and was ravenous. I knew the perfect solution to my hunger, though I would not give into it until I knew, for sure, that Damian would not wake up. So, I waited. I sat in my chair and stared at Damian. I hoped that he would wake up. I needed him to wake up, but if Damian did not wake up revenge would be mine.

***

I sat in the chair, staring at Damian, all night. I watched the time slowly tick away. The seven day mark was seconds away. I ran to Damian's bed. I leaned over him. I grabbed him by both arms. I started shaking him. Screaming at him.

"Wake up! Wake up! Please, Damian, don't leave me! Wake up! WAKE UP!!!!" I just kept yelling at him, hoping he would wake up. It was now past the seven day mark. I looked at the clock on the nightstand. It had to be fast. Minutes passed and soon an hour. I couldn't give up.

I heard someone enter the room. From her scent, I could tell it was my mother. I felt her grab my arm, trying to turn me away from Damian. Trying to get me out of the room.

The entire time she was doing this, I was shaking Damian and begging him to wake up. I heard my mother yell for my father. I heard him enter. A moment later, I felt arms around my waist. My father had lifted me off of Damian and was carrying me from the room.

"No, let me go! He will wake up! Damian will wake up!" I kept yelling at my father. I scratched and bit at any available surface. My father still held onto me. He wouldn't let me go.

After a few seconds, my father had me in the hallway, and the door to Damian was closed.

My father let me go. He stood in front of the door, so I couldn't get back in. I dropped to the floor, screaming and crying. Why had this happened to us? After everything I had been through, why take away the one person who meant the most in the World to me? This question brought up thoughts of Carter and the role he played in my life. He is the one who locked me up for years. He is the one who sent me away to the Human Lands. He is the one who did this to Damian. On this thought, my hybrid came forward. **They** wanted this just as much as I did. We needed it. We were connected in our need for revenge. I no longer thought of **them** as my monster. I was the monster all along.

In that moment, my entire demeanor changed. I stopped screaming. I stopped crying. My mind was void of all emotion, except rage. My fangs and claws were out. All three of *us* were forward. One cohesive unit.

I stood up and startled my father.

"Ava...?" He said, before he saw my face and eyes. He took a step back. He could tell that I was out for blood and I wouldn't stop. I turned and ran, as fast as I could. My father couldn't stop me. His werewolf speed was nowhere near as fast as my vampire sprint.

The Guard had the doors to the house blocked. They thought it was to keep everyone else out, but, at this moment, it was keeping me in. My mother had told me that the Guard did not watch the tunnel, It was the way that my parents had been using to get between the Council building and here. Now, it was my way to revenge.

I could hear my father behind me. Since I had stopped, he was slowly gaining on me. I quickly rectified that. I sped down the stairs and through the tunnel. my mother was preoccupied with Damian. If she had not been, she could have easily caught up to me.

My father made it to the tunnel, just as I went through the other side. I knew he would follow me and try to stop me. I took one last look at him before I closed the tunnel door. I pushed as much stuff as I could gather against the door, it would take awhile for him to get through.

Just as I was leaving the room, I heard him start to bang on the door. Using all of his strength trying to open it. My father begged me not to do what he knew I was planning, but I was too far gone.

I could smell Carter in the dungeons. There were not many Guard members inside of the building. They never expected a threat from the inside. It was their biggest weakness. I passed many Guard members without them noticing, they were all too busy socializing with one another, celebrating the new leadership. I made it to the stairs that led down to the dungeon with no problem. My prey was within my reach. I walked down gingerly, knowing that Carter could smell me coming. I was relishing in the fact that I could smell fear radiating off of him. He knew I could kill him and, now, he knew I would.

The Guard member that was in charge of watching Carter was at the bottom of the steps. He was a young werewolf. As soon as he saw me, he abandoned Carter. He must have heard what I had done to Carter before, and wanted no part of what was about to happen.

Carter was locked in a cell on the end. It was dark in the dungeon, but I could make him out in the back of his cell. He was cowering in the corner, visibly shaking. This once almighty man was now trembling beneath my might. I felt powerful! I felt dominant! I was now in control! I stalked up to his cage, feeling every bit the predator. The cage that he was in was supposed to be supernatural proof. I had no keys to open it, they had been attached to the fleeing guard. In my enraged state, I hadn't thought of that. I had to try and force myself into this cage. All I cared about, in that moment, was getting to Carter.

I grabbed the bars and began to pull as hard as I could, they wouldn't budge. I kept pulling. I was too angry to give up.

Carter began to relax. He came out of his crouched position in the corner, even dared to move closer to the bars. Closer to me.

I started looking for another way in, a key, anything!

"Aw! Is little Avalonia, giving up so soon? You just got started. Are you sure you don't want to try pulling on the bars some more?" Carter taunted and, as he did so, he got closer, and closer, to the bars. His confidence was growing. "Look, I am right here!" He said, as he stepped up to the bars.

As soon as I saw he was there, I launched myself forward. He tried to back up when he realized his mistake, but he was too late. Reaching through the gaps in the bars, I finally had my hands on him again, and this time I was not going to let him go. I pulled him closer, his face pushed up against the bars. I was too angry to speak. At this point, I was running on the base instincts of my hybrid self. I was truly a monster, one that, in that moment, I didn't mind being.

I smirked wickedly at him. I had one hand on the front of his shirt holding him in place, the other I slowly moved up to his neck. I took pleasure in torturing him. I was purposefully making it take as long as possible. I wanted him to suffer. The same way that I had suffered over that past week, while my mate lay dead, on the bed, in front of me.

I could hear footsteps on the stairs. I knew I needed to hurry, just a bit, if I wanted to kill him without interference. My hand on his neck began to squeeze. I gently let my hand that was gripping his shirt go, bringing it up to join the other, and squeezed even harder. His face was turning red from the struggle of trying to breathe. Blood was beginning to stain his shirt. My claws had broken skin.

The footsteps drew closer. I tightened my grip. I wanted to kill him. I needed to kill him! I was watching the life slowly leave his eyes, when I was suddenly pulled backward and thrust onto the ground. I lost my hold on Carter. A piece of his neck was still in my hand, attached to my claws. Since he was a werewolf and the wound was small he healed quickly. I bounded up, not caring, or bothering to notice, who had pulled me off, and made my way back to the cage. I could hear Carter gasping for breath, he had dragged himself back into the corner. He left a trail and blood was pooling around him. I knew I would not be able to trick him into coming to the bars again. My anger boiled over.

I turned to whoever had pulled me away from him. My anger now turned to them. How dare someone stop me from getting revenge!

My eyesight blurred with rage, adding to the darkness of the dungeon. This meant that I had to rely on my sense of smell. I turned in my new victim's direction. I could tell it was a vampire, but one whose scent I didn't recognize. My anger had so fully consumed me at this point, that I didn't care who it was. All I knew was that they had stopped me and, now, since I couldn't have Carter, they would have to do.

I didn't even think. I just lunged. I started biting and clawing at anything I could get my fangs and claws on. Whoever it was, they weren't fighting back. That made me angrier. Through my haze, I could barely hear my latest victim talking. It was a voice that sounded familiar, but it couldn't be. I kept hitting, trying to get the haunting voice to stop, but no matter how many times I would hit, it never would. I slowly came out of my haze. I was trying to process this. I wanted to believe it was true, but I had given up hope. I closed my eyes. My hybrid senses as confused as my human sensibility. How could it be possible?

"Avalonia?" The voice said again.

My eyes refused to open, even when the victim grabbed a hold of me and pulled me into a hug. They held me tightly. I started to calm down. My fangs and claws retracted. I was in my human state again. My hybrid was ready to come forward at any moment though. In my confusion of trying to figure out what was going on, who this person was, I had forgotten all my anger, at least for the moment. After a few moments, I finally dared to open my eyes.

What greeted me was the sight of dried blood on a shirt. The same shirt I had been staring at for a week now. My eyebrows scrunched together as I tried to put all the pieces together. I couldn't comprehend how it was possible. It had been over seven days. No one had ever awoken, as far as we knew, after that mark. I had to be sure. I slowly moved my head from the chest. I looked up at the face. My mouth dropped open, forming an o. My heart started racing. Tears began to stream down my face. There, in front of me, was my mate, my Damian.

He was smiling down at me, as if he didn't have a care in the world. The same smile that always said 'I love you'. Blood was dripping out of the corner of his mouth. The tears streamed faster and I started to collapse. He caught me before I could hit the ground. He sat down on the floor, with me in his arms, just holding me as I cried. My arms were wrapped tightly around his neck, If he was still human, it would have strangled him.

"Avalonia?" Damian said.

I looked up at him. By this point, I was starting to smile, too.

"Are you going to be okay, now? If I let you up, you're not going to attack anyone?" He asked, with a slight smile.

I shook my head and tried not to laugh. He was asking how I was, after he had been considered dead this entire week. Now that I had my Damian, there was no need to kill. I had gotten my revenge by scaring Carter. He was still huddled in the corner, coughing and holding his neck. He shook anytime I looked his way.

I stood up and Damian followed.

"How?" I asked. "It had been seven days. No one has ever came back after that much time."

Damian looked down, my eyebrows went together in confusion.

"I am so sorry that you had to go through that..." He said.

I stuck my hand on the bottom of his chin and pulled his head up to look at me.

"How, in any way, is this your fault? If any one is to blame, it is Carter." I let out a growl his way, then turned back to Damian. "This was something you had no control over."

He looked at me, as a small smile graced his mouth. "That doesn't mean I can't feel bad about it." I opened my mouth to interrupt. He put a finger on my lips to silence me and continued. "I always will, because you were in pain this week. I just wish I could have been here to help. To answer your question about waking up after the seven day mark, I don't know how it happened. I was laying there, in nothingness, when I heard you crying. I fought to get to you, and I woke up. Then, I got out of bed and went to the door. I had no idea what was going on. I opened the door and your mother was there. She was leaning against the wall. Tears in her eyes. I startled her when I spoke. She explained to me what was going on. She told me how I am now a vampire and about you coming down here. I knew I had to stop you from doing something you would regret. Something that you would never do otherwise."

I pulled him into a hug and held him. I had missed being this close to him. I let go after a few moments and stepped back, so I could look at him. The transformation into a vampire had changed him only slightly. His skin was lighter but, other than that, he had stayed the same.

"I am sorry I wasn't there when you woke up. They dragged me from the room. I just became so angry. I kept thinking of how, because of Carter, you were having to go through the change into a vampire, or worse, you had died. As the days went on, I got angrier. Until, finally, I snapped." I said.

He grabbed my hand, then put his other hand on the side of my face and kissed me. It was magical. When he kissed me, my lips began to tingle. He ran his hands along my sides and my back. Everywhere he touched it felt like sparks of electricity. My body grew weak with the sensations bombarding it.

Damian pulled away from the kiss. With a look of astonishment, he said, "This is amazing! I knew that vampires could sense their soulmates, but, as a human, I never understood what that meant. Now, as a vampire... It has shown me, physically, what I already knew to be true, emotionally... You are my soul mate! The one I am meant to spend everyday of the rest of my life with! All of the feelings I had for you seem to be amplified! Before, I knew it in my heart, but now... It's like I can feel it in my soul! At the very core of me. We are one..."

With that said, we kissed again. This time seemed even more special. Damian could finally feel what I felt. He now knew how powerful my feelings were, and, in return, he experienced the same feelings. The magnetism that we shared locked us together in that moment. It felt as if we shared each other's hearts. As if our very souls were now in sync.

We were startled out of that moment by the sound of a throat clearing behind us. We separated to see my parents there. They both had smiles on their faces and tears in their eyes. It was the first time I had ever seen my strong Alpha father cry. They came forward and hugged us both.

Chapter 28

My screams rang throughout the house. Damian was by my side in an instant. It had been five years since he had become a vampire. During that time; we had gotten married, had our mating ceremony, and became Súmaire and Súmaise to the coven. Now, I was about to give birth to our first child.

My parents and newborn, wolf-cub baby brother were in the other room, all waiting to see what my child would be.

I had been in labor for hours. This child was stubborn. I guess he had to be, with parents like Damian and me. I grabbed Damian's hand, once again, as pain ripped through me. It wouldn't be long now. The doctor told me to push. So, I did. Three pushes later and our son was here! Our Dimitri.

Cassandra, and the witch doctor who was helping with the birth, took him into a little room, off to the side, to check him over and find out what species he would be. My heart was pounding. I was beyond nervous. Would he be a hybrid and have to go through the same things I did? Would he be a werewolf? A vampire? I even considered the possibility that he would be human, maybe even have some witch in him. I was wringing my hands intently. I kept gripping the sheets, to the point that I eventually ripped them. After that, Damian grabbed my hand and held it. He tried to calm me down, even though he was just as nervous. He had been standing outside the door to the room they were in, trying to hear anything they said, but it was fruitless. They were speaking so low that even his vampire hearing couldn't pick it up.

Five minutes had past when Cassandra and the doctor returned. Both were smiling. As soon as the door opened, Damian jumped up.

"Is he okay? What is he?" Damian asked, as soon as he saw them.

"Relax, Damian. Let me give the baby to Avalonia, then he will tell both of you." Cassandra said.

Cassandra handed Dimitri over to me, then stepped back. The doctor came and stood in front of me and Damian.

"Neither of you have anything to worry about. Your son is perfectly healthy." He paused. My heart rate spiked. "He is a vampire." He said.

I began to cry in joy. My baby boy, my son, would be able to have a normal, vampire, life. Damian came over and hugged me, and we both looked at our son, as Cassandra and the doctor left the room.

My life had changed a lot over the years. I went from being afraid of who, and what, I was, to finally embracing all that I am. My hybrid nature now gives me strength. Through it all, I finally worked out the inner turmoil of my mind, body, and spirit. Now "**they**" have become some of the best parts of **me**.

As I look back on my life, I know that I would not change a thing. All of the pain and struggles that I went through led me to where I am, now. By embracing, and coming to fully understand, the *darkness* inside of me, I found my light. This is not the full story of my life, but it is the part I cherish most, the part that made me whole.